- to make
an underworld

Robert Escrick was a good name. It was even Sir Robert Escrick Cravenhead's own — or part of it. So when the former chairman of the family firm ('Cravenhead's means machine tools') decided to disappear, because the firm had been taken over, he was retiring early, and his wife was abroad and no longer noticed whether he was around or not, it seemed to him entirely natural to adjust his name and set off for Cornwall, accompanied only by Banjo, his dog.

There was a house waiting for him in Cornwall — one he had had built in readiness. There was also a strange young woman waiting for him, locked in the bathroom and claiming to have been raped. Admittedly she was feeble-minded, but the locals took her part against a newcomer, and Robert found himself an object of suspicion from the start. Of course there were compensations: freedom to read and go long walks with Banjo; the charming artist Nesta Clare; the enigmatic Roundstone and his boat (what did he do, anchored offshore for hours on end? Not fishing.) Robert found it easy to ignore appeals in the agony columns of the London papers, asking him to get in touch.

And then the feeble-minded girl was found murdered, and realities impinged on Robert's retreat — realities connected with Roundstone which Robert could not afford to ignore.

by the same author

-to make
an underworld

by Joan Fleming

G. P. Putnam's Sons
New York

FIRST AMERICAN EDITION 1976

COPYRIGHT © 1976 BY JOAN FLEMING

SBN: 399-11809-8

Library of Congress Cataloging in Publication Data

Fleming, Joan Margaret.
    To make an underworld.

    (Red mask mystery)
    I. Title.
PZ3.F62845Tm3   [PR6011.L46]   823'.9'14   76-14808

Portion of "mehitabel again" from the book *archy's life of mehitabel* by Don Marquis, copyright ©
1933 by Doubleday & Company, Inc. Later appeared in *the lives and times of archy and mehitabel*.
Reprinted by permission of Doubleday & Company, Inc.

PRINTED IN THE UNITED STATES OF AMERICA

CHAPTER I

THE NEW CHAIRMAN, being a member of one of the top ten livery companies of the City of London and an Alderman, had arranged that some thirty chosen people should have luncheon in that Company's Hall in the City after the last Annual General Meeting of the firm of Cravenhead had taken place and the shareholders had said what they wished to say about the take-over.

Well, not all they wished to say, but they were allowed to say enough to indicate that the gist was in favour, if not enthusiastic. Of course, every single one who stood up to speak, started with regret that the old name of this famous firm should be 'merged', as it was euphemistically called. *Cravenhead's means machine tools* had been the cry. But Cravenhead's, in order to keep going at their previous rate of output, needed the firm who were taking over, more than it needed its – as some put it – cracked name.

The retiring chairman, Robert Escrick Cravenhead, great-grandson of the firm's founder in Lancashire, was now completely relaxed; after the oysters he sat picking his teeth entirely unnecessarily, and thoughtfully. He would prefer to have another half-dozen oysters and nothing more to eat, but that was out of the question.

He did not know the man on his left but he glanced at him; as the retiring chairman, who had made his dynamic farewell speech, he did not want to have any small talk with the man sitting on his left but that man was waiting to catch his eye and said what he had clearly rehearsed in advance: 'So the mantle of Elijah is fallen upon Elisha, Sir Robert!' It was a good opening, but Robert had resolved never again to strive to make an intentional witty remark so he simply nodded and smiled while he tried hard to remember if he had put the groundsheet in the back of the Range Rover as he had finally packed it up before anyone was about this morning. He might well

need it to cover the logs in winter time, keeping them dry
for the fine blazes he intended to make in that grand open
grate.

His neighbours on either side, indeed, both of them
ex-Lord Mayors of London, knew only too well how he
was feeling and spared him by making only the simplest
form of conversation, and the new chairman of the firm,
now called Crown, Weston & Co. Ltd, evidently a
sensitive man, broke up the luncheon-party as soon as his
guests were adequately fed; there had been enough
speeches for one day.

At the door, the hall porter handed Robert his bowler
hat. 'You can keep it,' Robert said as he waved it away
and then spoiled his gesture by adding: '. . . for funerals.'

'Thank you, sir . . . a taxi?'

No, not a taxi. Days ago Robert had found himself a
lock-up garage belonging to a surgeon at St Bartholomew's
Hospital whom he knew vaguely and whom he had
persuaded to lend him the private garage for twelve hours
while the surgeon was going abroad for a short visit.

If it had been warm he could have taken off his coat,
but there was an icy May wind blowing and a fish-white
sky above. As he backed out of the garage there was a
disarrangement amongst the goods and baggage he had
so carefully built up in the back of the Range Rover; it
was packed to the roof by the time he had finished at six
a.m. He hoped it would all stay put till he reached his
destination. When he got back into the car after locking
the door of the garage, there was another lurch of the
goods.

As he drove to the main entrance of the hospital to
leave the key at the desk he reminded himself that here
was a man who, from this moment onwards, was dedicated to a life without the luxury of service, now fussing
about the safety of the huge pile of *things* he was taking
with him. But then, he reminded himself, he had to have
music and he was entirely incapable of playing any
musical instrument at all; he could hardly rely on his
enjoyment of music if he merely sang to himself, and

without any printed music at that: so he had brought a variety of excellent quality hi-fi equipment.

There would be the gulls, and the sea, and the wind whistling round his new home in Cornwall, he thought, as he passed everybody on the Shepherd's Bush flyover. And he ought to do without this car too, if he were to be true to his aspirations; but since the cottage had no proper road but only a track to it, the Range Rover was essential, it would seem.

The car was brand new and he must remember not to go too fast, though it was a delight to drive; even at ninety he felt he was keeping to the latest speed limit of fifty (under the saving petrol scheme). He must take care not to relax too much or he would forget to stop and go shooting off the final edge of his country at Land's End.

At Zennor he slowed down to thirty and kept to that speed along the narrow roads. What he was about to achieve was a way of life the plans for which had kept him cool and amiable over the last two grilling years of hard work, and now he was on the very edge of achievement he was filled with foreboding.

He had flown, without even his secretary knowing, five times from London to Newquay and back and the last time was two days before Christmas where he had met the builders' architect and discussed the finishing touches. Since then he had been unable to leave and the cottage was supposed to be ready for him. What if he found the builders and their material still there and mistakes made in all directions?

It was very nearly dark when he started to look out for the opening which led to his new home along a track which was hardly worthy of the name; half a mile long from the gateless opening from the road.

He arrived, stopped, turned on the headlights which flooded the front of the long converted coastguard's cottage with its stone-tiled roof. Bless it, it had retained its appearance almost as it had looked from the first, in spite of everything that had been done to it. He took out the sacred key and put it in the lock, but as he was doing so there was a noise from behind and, turning, he saw packages, bedclothes and his sleeping-bag slipping about; he also saw a familiar sight as his black labrador Banjo sprang over to the driving seat and jumped out, triumphant.

He might have known it; Banjo had planned this as carefully as he himself had planned his secret getaway. Early this morning after he started to pack up with everything he planned to bring, his tool-box, his Calor gas grill, his radio, his boots, his bedclothes and his books, he had looked round for his friend Banjo and he was nowhere to be seen. He shouted and whistled at the risk of the gardener and his wife hearing from their cottage behind the stables. Then he went round the house looking for the dog; it had never for a moment occurred to him that he should take Banjo, whose job was to protect the house.

Banjo had always understood that the beloved master was only available at times, but this morning at six a.m. there had been a change in the air; packing his boots was different for one thing and indicated country hiking, and while the master was looking round the house for him he had concealed himself beneath the pile of bedclothes that had been put on top of everything else, the bedclothes, in fact, in which the master had slept last night.

So Robert, having a final look round to see if he had left anything he intended to take, felt wretched; he had never once thought of taking him because it would mean leaving him in the car from six a.m. to three p.m., unattended in the City of London. Since he could not find him the question seemed to have answered itself and he drove the first ten miles to London miserably.

Banjo sprang up and licked his face, refrained from knocking him down and dashed wildly about, only stopping for seconds to lift his leg; he had been eighteen hours without doing this so he must have been aware of what was going to happen and refrained from his usual long early morning drink. Robert laughed out loud and hugged Banjo to him and the dog responded in full. Only he knew how important he was going to be to his master, who was clearly delighted to have him there. 'But let's go in,' Banjo begged, 'because I'm hungry and I need some grub.'

Robert had no intention of unpacking tonight, he had purposely put the things he would immediately need at the ready on the passenger seat; the large shopping basket containing coffee, eggs, bread and bacon, and the gas container, the change of clothes . . . he went across to the front door in the glare of the headlights and tried to turn the key, but it was already unlocked.

He had his first twinge of annoyance to find it unlocked, but when he went in, turned on his torch and looked round the room he grunted with satisfaction and the warmth which greeted him told him that the builders had paid attention to his last instructions as to when he was arriving and lighted the solid fuel Aga cookery-stove.

This was at the kitchen-end of the long living-room, the huge fireplace at the opposite end with a door beside it which led to the bedroom and the bathroom. He walked across the room, lighted by the headlights from the car. He opened the door, and put his hand on the latch of the second door immediately inside, which opened into the bathroom.

Now the bathroom was going to be Robert's pride and joy. There had been a nasty scullery, stone-built from at least a hundred years ago, jutting out from the back; it had a mean little window and a rusty corrugated-iron roof. 'We'll make it into a decent bathroom,' the architect assured him. But wait a minute; the stonework was in perfect condition. 'It'll have to come down, of course,' the architect had said, 'to make room for a good big bath.' But Robert knew what he wanted: 'I don't need a bath, they are enervating, I only use a shower. It will take a shower easily.' It was obvious that it would take a shower but Robert was a tall man and the shower would have to be sunk slightly into the floor. He had a much better idea: glass bricks for a flat roof and a self-propelled ventilator for the tiny window! When he had done some measuring the architect rather grudgingly agreed that it was a splendid idea, he rather wished he had thought of it himself, but the next client . . .

So now Robert irritably rattled the new decorative iron latch up and down and swore; it was bolted inside, but how could it be?

It would only be bolted inside if whoever had bolted it were inside too.

Banjo was gasping with excitement and joy; the master was pleased, his plan had succeeded, he was welcome; his excited breathing could have been heard a hundred yards off. Robert put his hand on Banjo's black head: 'Shh . . .' He stood absolutely motionless and Banjo did likewise. For a full minute they stood, ears pricked for the slightest sound.

Then Robert went back to the car and pulled out the provision basket, turned off the headlights and returned to the living-room, took out two candles from the basket and lighted them with the box of matches he had left ready in the car days ago, in case he forgot. He had bought two cheap enamel candlesticks too, of the kind the Victorians called chamber, of the correct shape to carry upstairs to bed. Carrying one, he went to the bathroom door and looked at it carefully; it was an oak door, as he had ordered, and it seemed to fit perfectly so that if there was anyone inside they would probably not see a glimmer of light showing through.

Then he snatched at the iron catch and furiously rattled it up and down, so that anybody inside could not fail to hear the noise. He heard a sound. A voice. He stopped rattling and listened hard. He started rattling again and went on for a good minute. Then stopped.

He indistinctly heard a screeching voice, probably asking who was there.

Only in the nick of time did he remember that he was no longer Robert Cravenhead to people he met from now on, but Robert Escrick, which he had in fact been christened, with the Cravenhead to follow, but now to be obliterated.

'It's Robert Escrick,' he shouted.

While he waited for the expected question: Who are you? he thought he could take the candle round the back and, holding it to his face, he could show himself through the automatic ventilator or even see the face inside, but he instantly dismissed that idea because if any faces were to be visible, the ventilator would have to be revolving at top speed and if it were doing that, the flame of the candle would be blown out; in any case, there was not much wind.

There was no reply and Robert retreated to one of the rocking-chairs beside the fireplace, pulled it round to face the bathroom door and sat down to think.

It was quarter to eleven on the evening of the May day upon which he had planned to disappear from every aspect of the life he had always led, and start again, a new person. No, perhaps not, the same person with a new name. It had been a long and full day, at the end of which he was hoping to unpack the car to the extent he needed to, lock his door and go to bed, where he had assumed, without any doubt whatever, he was going to have a good long sleep.

So what was the best thing to do now? In his bathroom was a woman with a weak voice and an unfamiliar accent, perhaps, but that was only guesswork since he had only heard what amounted to unconnected words.

Banjo was ravenous, but when the master was thinking, he knew better than to mention his own needs; with a slight groan he settled himself down on the new elm floor which was not too cold.

'Why the hell didn't I have a lock fitted instead of the primitive latch and bolt? A lock could be dealt with from outside but nothing can be done about the bolt; even the frailest little bolts stand up to immense pressure and that *olde Englishe bolt* would withstand a bull-dozer almost.'

He sat for another ten minutes; he rocked gently in this splendid modern rocking-chair of which he had bought two and he felt the relaxation which he had intended, even in this awkward situation. So much so that he decided that this problem had better be put off till morning; come the daylight all would be solved. Perhaps she would have slipped out.

So he got up and so did Banjo, so excitedly that he was obliged to take out the wholemeal loaf and give him the lot. 'I'm sorry, old man,' he said once or twice, 'no meat, but I'll make up for it tomorrow.'

At the kitchen-end was a sink unit, a set of drawers and counter, modern in concept but made entirely by hand and of modern oak rather than the pine used all over the place these days. He fitted the little gas cooker in the place intended for it, and the cylinder of gas with the rubber tube leading to it, below the counter. He turned it on and it worked; he took his coffee-pot and filled the percolator with coffee and put it on a low light where it blobbed slowly, making his coffee which he must always have in the morning, the instant he woke up. He found the whisky bottle and poured some into one of the thick glasses they always took for picnics.

He brought in the bedclothes and the pillows and threw them on the built-against-the-wall bed. He was still wearing the suit in which he had spent this important day, and even though he was starting this new life he could not allow himself to sleep in it. He took it off and hung it up in the built-in cupboard, on the hanger he had brought with him. He dragged out his very old cords and put them on with a thick polo-necked jersey. He began to whistle. He had another glass of whisky and looked to see if Banjo had left any bread. He had not; the dog had now gone out to explore the wide open spaces. Robert ate a goodly hunk of real Cheddar cheese and felt quite inordinately happy.

It was the whisky, of course, but it was other things too. He was here! It was that it had actually happened, and he had never really thought it would: he might have had a sudden coronary and died; he might have been run over as he crossed Princes Street to the luncheon; he might have been killed in a multiple accident on the motorway as he drove down. In that case he would be dead and his family would be bound to know all about his secretive plans and how petty they would seem; how shocked they would be that he spent so much care and paid so much attention to his own comfort.

When people of sense, like, he hoped, himself decide to opt out, disappear, start a new life shedding all their previous commitments, friends, relations, dogs, the lot, they should do it with some kind of panache, swagger, style. Here in Cornwall he was no more inaccessible than he would have been at Kingston upon Thames. It was laughable, really, and he laughed.

Well, he was known as a cheerful man on the whole, he laughed quite a bit in the ordinary way, but during these last two or three years there had not been anything to laugh at and he had felt himself developing the dry, unamused, typical businessman's hoot.

He had now lighted two more candles and, looking round his living-room, he laughed for pure and simple joy because it was so nice. The huge old refectory table he had bought in an auction at an old house near them in the country, one day when his wife was away; the twin benches that an antique-dealer had found for him, the two brand new rocking-chairs; they were exactly how he wished, the old blending with the brand new, and before going to bed he closed all the shutters which was the ultimate pleasure. Even his room at Oxford, forty years ago, had not given him so much pleasure.

He blew out all the candles but one and lay in his bed waiting for Banjo to come in. He thought about the infestation in the bathroom, he could not take it seriously. Today was the day he reckoned to have stopped taking things seriously. Right, there was a woman or girl in the bathroom, locked herself in. The bathroom door was at right angles to the bedroom door, inside the bedroom, and his bed was against the wall at the end of the twenty-two-feet-or-so long room.

Nobody other than an individual like Robert would settle for simply leaving her there and going off to sleep. Maybe she would creep out and away, once he slept, and he left the bedroom door open with this in mind.

Or maybe not. But what else could he do but go to sleep? The nearest help of any kind could possibly be a good two miles and he was far too tired to drive off to seek someone with a tool suitable for opening bolted doors. There was no telephone, nor did he intend to have one fitted.

Of course, he had his own tool-box but . . . no, he also had Banjo and Banjo's whole existence was built upon his genius at frightening people out of their wits, if required to do so. He had never in his whole life bitten anybody because he had never had the need; if he was on guard he had only to snarl, or even to bark, to cause people to disappear over the horizon at top speed. He had one of those very low-pitched black, black barks which most evidently cried havoc.

He was getting sleepy; without the menace in the bathroom, he would have left the front door ajar and let Banjo come home and lie down to sleep when he was tired of exploring, but now common sense made him get up and stagger to the door, whistle off and on for a minute, pat Banjo for being a good obedient boy coming when summoned, see him settled in front of the Aga and return to bed. This certainly meant that the bathroom occupant was not going to slip out unobserved; it was doubtful if Banjo would keep her trapped inside or rush out barking at her heels if she defied him at the door.

The last thing he thought before sleep overcame him was that if the bathroom door opened in the morning and there was nobody inside, he must have started hallucinations due to pressure of work; he had often thought he might.

CHAPTER II

WHEN HE WOKE at a quarter to eight, three-quarters of an hour beyond his usual waking-time, he had forgotten about the bathroom problem; he leaped out of bed and flung open the shutters and before him was spread the feast of reasons why he had come and his face bore traces of the small boy gazing with delight upon his Christmas parcels spread out for him beneath the Christmas tree. A small red sail was placed in the exact centre of the horizon, like the cherry in the middle of the cake for fun. It was as though the whole scene had been prepared for his delight, washed and polished, and he stood beating his bare chest with both hands and smiling delightedly; he must take it all in now because these fabulous mornings, more often than not, did not last.

When he had to go to the bathroom he raised the latch, forgetting, and cursed loudly because it still did not open. He listened acutely with his ear close to the door. 'Are you there?'

There was some kind of reply, faint.

'Speak up, I can't hear.'

There were more sounds which were unidentifiable.

'I say – ' he raised his voice – 'if you're in trouble I dare say I can help if you will unbolt the door.' He waited and repeated three times, loud and clear as though addressing an idiot: 'Unbolt the door!' He had not tried the bolt inside because it had not been fitted when he was last down; the architect had simply showed him what he called 'the luxury door furniture' in excellent quality decorative black iron, and surely luxury door furniture should present no problem of opening. In a few moments after his last clear instructions to unbolt he heard the bolt being slowly pulled back and when the sound stopped he pulled up the latch and pushed the door open. There should, of course, have been a beautiful naked damsel reclining, but there was not; in any case, it would have been extremely difficult to recline at all in that small square space. The ventilator was blowing slowly round but did not prevent the stuffy, fusty smell which was clearly caused by the pathetic bundle crouching at his feet.

'Idiot!' he had thought a few seconds ago.

She was a girl of sorts in an exceedingly weak state. She was wearing a very old leather coat, thick stockings and shoes which were much too big for her, and when she tried to stand up she clearly could not. He bent down and scooped her up and carried her to his bed, where he laid her down gently and arranged her arms and legs decently so that he might survey her.

'Twitty Woo!' he said unexpectantly. Twitty Woo was a village idiot at Robert's old home in Westmorland and his first friend. He had surveyed her from his pram at the age of three and had been puzzled because she was different from other people in the village; their dog always barked madly whenever they met; he and Nanny used to aim blows at the dog with her umbrella. And one day she said to the gardener's wife who happened to be walking to the village with her: 'Aren't dogs funny? They always know and bark hysterically when anybody's different.'

This Northern idiot of Robert's youth was not by any means unpleasant to look at but she moved strangely with her legs curled round at twenty-five past six. She always seemed to have her hair in curlers and her face wore an expression which was a mixture of suspicion, shyness and sly. Later Robert saw her very often in church with her hair out of pins; it was golden and curly and fell around her shoulders. As she wandered about, sometimes with wild flowers in her hands, or carrying a very long black silk cat, she would make a noise in imitation of an owl. In later life when Robert would sometimes return to his family village to visit the aged parents, Twitty Woo was still around and seemed hardly to have aged at all; the grown-up Robert had often thought what a splendid Ophelia she would have made. The reason she appeared not to have aged was that her hair had the same quality but it was pale silver instead of pale gold, and since her mind was a blank she had no lines upon her face.

Leaving this brand new Twitty Woo upon the bed, he went to turn on the gas to heat up the coffee he had made last night and sat in one of his new rocking-chairs to think as he drank it. There was no problem, really.

He would have to find out from the builders where they kept the second lot of keys and why the door had been left unlocked. Perhaps it was because they had forgotten to instruct the men on the site regarding the exact time of the new owner's arrival.

The girl would have wandered along the shore from Carrioth, which was the nearest village and three miles away. It would have been easier and shorter by at least a mile to come by the sands and not along the winding road from the village. There was a twisting footpath up from the shore to the long low cottage where the Admiralty policeman had lived for a century or so, now being converted into a dwelling, and no doubt she was curious to see what the workmen had been doing with it all this time.

But, of course, why lock herself in the bathroom and stay there for, perhaps, several days? To judge from her weakness she might have been there more than a day, even up to a week!

Having finished his coffee he was full of energy, ideas, resource and efficiency; he would deal with this strange little problem with expertise, in the absence of any more important problem, for once. Well, he had another problem which he had put off till this actual day and it was what he was going to do about his wife Angela, who was at present having a holiday with her sister who lived in Sardinia. He would gladly put forward the Angela question yet again, he had intended writing to her as soon as she had left home two weeks ago but somehow . . . he had had a lot in hand!

He made some toast and buttered a slice which he took in to Twitty Woo on a plate; he sat down on the bed and

took a piece between his fingers and offered it with his
kind smile. A shadow of a smile flickered across her face
and she reached out for it. It was soon eaten and he went
to pour out a mug of coffee; that, too, was acceptable.

He picked up the clothes he had thrown about last
night and disappeared into the bathroom with them. Soon
there was the sound of the shower and the girl, looking
much better, pulled herself up and, supported by her
elbows, she looked round the room and seemed assured.

Returning, Robert brushed his hair in front of the built-
in looking-glass above the built-in dressing chest, admir-
ing each item of furniture as he did so, then turned round
and with the utmost kindness addressed himself to the
waif.

Getting information out of her was not easy but it was
possible, particularly if you were someone who could so
readily inspire confidence as Robert. She wanted to
please him, to take the puzzled look off his face and cause
the smile to appear that showed he was pleased. She
strove, it was clear, to please.

What was perfectly clear was that there had been something, somebody or some event that she had found
intolerable. Whatever it was had frightened her very
much indeed. She might well have died there in Robert's
bathroom, alone, rather than have had the experience
repeated. All the artifice that the young Robert had
devised for communication with his childhood friend
Twitty Woo came flowing back to him over the years in
the weirdest way. He could make her understand what he
wished to say, but of course, to cause her to make him
understand in return was a great deal more difficult. It
did not seem possible for her to tell him how many days
she had been in the bathroom nor what manner of horror
had caused her to act as she did, but she left him fully
aware of the seriousness of whatever it was that had
happened.

He soon felt she was tiring, her eyes started to slither
away from him and she sank back against the pillows.

He told her he would now go and take out and put

away all the household things he had packed into the car and when he had tidied up he would take her into the village and she would point out to him where she lived with her mother? Sister? Brother? Aunt? No answer.

He then went into his new bathroom and examined it carefully. It was quite lethal, he decided. The glass-block roof had been partly his idea and partly the architect's. The latter was a pleasant young man called Jack Wither, delighted that his services had been required by someone who had the money to carry out all the ideas that he had to keep in cold storage in this unproductive countryside. The glass bricks had been fitted into a specially made iron frame and dropped over the walls like a lid on a storage jar. There should have been a bigger window but the ventilator fitted the old window space to perfection and seemed to be working admirably in its own draught; the walls and floor were beautifully tiled in sea-green tiles, there was no frame or curtain, simply the tiled floor with a drain like a pavement drain and a spray fixed on the wall, with an arm stretching out over the customer splashing about below. Delightful. But what about anyone locking themselves in and fire raging through the cottage?

If the fire inspector called he could condemn the bathroom. But there was, of course, an easy answer: for the bathroom door to be fitted with a proper means of opening and shutting, not with the primitive and pretentious countrified iron latch but with two glass knobs and a keyhole straight through. And it would not be a bad idea to have a more fragile door, one you could kick down if necessary instead of a modern 'luxury' one, three inches thick, guaranteed not to start burning in case of direct flame for forty-five minutes.

An hour passed before he was ready to leave. He saw she lay just as he had left her, almost lifeless. He leaned over and looked at her and she cringed away as though in fear. He did not want to lift her up and carry her but he could see no alternative; wasting no time over it, he did just that and dumped her on the passenger seat. Then he shut all the windows, locked the front door and jumped in the car beside her. Under the circumstances, he explained to Banjo, he could not come but must stay here and guard.

With a population of two and a half thousand, Carrioth did not have a police station of any stature; there was a sergeant in charge, however, and he was sitting at his desk with his hat beside him when Robert entered and there was a strong smell of boiling cabbage. Robert always felt slight embarrassment when talking to a hatless bobby; he felt even more so this morning with: 'I've got this girl in the car, Officer. I don't know whether she's a native of this village or not but when I arrived from London last night she was locked in my bathroom.'

'Your name, sir?'

'Robert Escrick, I bought a coastguard's cottage up there, Zoygate. I've been having it repaired and so on this last year and I've come down now to take it over. The builders are Brown & Bright of Penzance and the architect is Jack Wither. They were informed a week or so ago that I was coming, I wrote to them myself, told them to have the stove lighted and gave them the date . . .'

He realized as he was talking what an extraordinary story he had to tell. He found his front door shut, unlocked, no key and there was a girl in a locked bathroom!

The sergeant was making notes and now he put down his pen and looked squarely at Robert. 'Crum,' he said, announcing his name, and then: 'How long has she been there?'

'How can I know? The door had a bolt inside, last night there was no getting her to pull it back. I simply had to leave things as they were. It was late and there is no electric light. This morning, she's very feeble but she did succeed in pulling the bolt back and letting me in. I'd say she's been there twenty-four hours, possibly even several days . . .'

Wordless, the sergeant put on his hat and went outside. The girl was lying sideways now, unable to keep herself upright; the sergeant opened the door and pulled her upright. 'There, there!' he comforted as she let out a small scream. 'Not to take on, you're home and dry.' He pointed to some cottages beyond the small row of shops. 'She lives there. What's to do, Biddy?'

She moaned and shook her head.

He turned to Robert: 'She's a bit . . .' He tapped his head. 'It's Biddy Hallow; she lives with her grandmother. She wanders about all day long, mostly on the shore, collecting shells. She makes these shell boxes, y'know . . . all stuck over with shells, like. Her grandmother's a bit of a . . . well, y'know . . . nutcase too. Why didn't she report Biddy missing? She's done this afore, quite often, I'd say, but never for long. You think she was in your bathroom as long as a week, sir?'

'To judge by her condition it could well have been a week, that is if she was a reasonably fit person in the ordinary way. She may have been shamming, of course.'

'Oh, she's physically fit all right, walks miles along the shore finding shells; she takes a rum old basket with her; quite picturesque, the tourists think; she's had dozens, hundreds of photographs taken with her basket on her arm and her hair all over the place. The sea maiden, one silly ass called her and asked her where her tail was. You'll have noticed her legs aren't quite . . . I reckon I dunno how she gets along at all. She's a donkey of her own but as often as not she leaves him at home.'

He removed his hat, scratched his head and put his hat back on. 'Well, I don't know . . . old Mrs Hallow goes to the parsonage all day, cooking and that, washing too. She's not back afore teatime any day except Sunday. I dunno . . . I reckon . . .'

He looked thoughtfully at Robert and Robert received his meaning; he hoped that Robert would drive round to the Parsonage and find Mrs Hallow. With rising irritation he opened the driving door and indicated to the sergeant that he had better climb in the back. But the sergeant was a busy man and could not leave his office and his telephone, with everything lying about all over the place.

He went back inside and Robert was left with the girl Biddy eyeing him. Eyeing him. In what way? Just plain eyeing.

He strolled up the village street and back; it was unprepossessing, sandy, a bit dull; everyone stared at him and he felt like a tourist, looked like one too, he had no doubt. He planned to use his old boots next time he came into the village, whitewash them first, take the laces out and bend the toes upwards, he might then fit into the picture better.

There was a butcher just down a side street, he needed meat not only for his lunch but for Banjo. He went in and came out with steak and a pound of mince; not having any electricity, he had no freezer and it was made clear to him now that he would have to come down to the village every day . . . or starve. He bought potatoes, onions, carrots, frozen peas; he put them in the back of the car. He stamped impatiently just as the sergeant emerged briskly from his now tidy office.

They were directed to the Parsonage by the sergeant leaning forward from the back and stating that the Parson would go stark staring mad if they went in round the front.

If Robert had been a wandering playwright collecting characters, he would no doubt have been enchanted by Mrs Hallow, but Robert was revolted. She was the awful crone from a Christmas pantomime, croaking out evil oaths and curses and vanquished in the end by the Good Fairy. She wanted to know where Biddy had been and why; how she got there and whom she had been with; and she behaved as though Robert and the sergeant were two vile miscreants.

'Now come along, missus. This gentleman has taken the trouble to bring your granddaughter home; he don't know more than any of us do. Now just be quiet and let us know what you want done with Biddy. Come along now, quick, we can't waste any more time. She's lying in this gentleman's motor-car, looks done up!'

Mrs Hallow said he must telephone for an ambulance

from Zennor; she wanted the girl examined, and the way she said it was pointed to the extent of being positively evil. Sergeant Crum, however had the measure of her; his manner became distinctly militant; he and this gentleman would lift Biddy inside the kitchen and leave her there and Mrs Hallow could do what she thought best because they could waste no more time, and, disregarding her protestations they did just that and drove away between the rhododendrons of the back drive with her injured jackdaw cries following them.

Back at the police station Robert did not get out of the car but the sergeant had not quite finished with him. He wanted an assurance that Robert would make enquiries from the builders and the architect as to what happened up at Zoygate; whether they knew anything about the girl Biddy or how she had had entry, as the sergeant called it, to the house. If the door had been locked when the men had last left the premises and whether anybody was seen around.

Robert made no promises but listened and nodded soberly; he said he would call as soon as he had the necessary information. He thanked the sergeant for his help.

Driving back, the morning was so beautiful that he laughed out loud. This was the kind of morning in Cornwall he had remembered all the years since he was a student, the kind of morning it was worth a very great deal to achieve and he had done it, even though he had waited forty years for it. It made him absurdly happy and he shouted and sang as he bumped and bounced over the rocky track with the lark singing gloriously, invisible in the blue, blue sky.

How could he fulfil Sergeant Crum's instructions? He thought there was no telephone-box up here and he was not going to make sure there was one. It meant posts and wires and it meant bills that he could not check for accuracy, but above all . . . it meant trouble. The telephone, if he had one, could not bring him glad tidings because the glad tidings were here and now, attainable

and attained. Any news would be bad news and he did
not want it. He did not need any of his business friends to
telephone because anything they wanted to say, they had
already said; he did not want to answer questions because
he had given all the answers at great length.

He wanted Banjo bounding out to greet him, which he
did, and he wanted to get that piece of steak on the grill as
soon as possible.

He quite definitely did not want that luxurious
Porsche waiting for him in the clearing in front of the
house. However, it turned out to belong to the ambitious
young architect, Jack Wither, who was at the back of
the house, lying flat and scraping away with his penknife at
a section of the damp course. He jumped to his feet and
dusted himself down.

'How do you like it, sir?'

Robert was sorry to damp down his enthusiasm by
saying that he had not, as yet, had time to look round,
but he told him about the bathroom episode which he
had only just been able to shake off, if shake it off he had,
and he wanted to know where the entrance door keys
were. He waved the two he had been sent and said that
when he arrived last night the door was shut but not
locked and no keys were around.

'The chaps knew you had your keys,' Jack Wither said,
his head almost hanging with disappointment that everything had not gone as smoothly as he had hoped. He had
taken great pains to see that all was as spick and span as
possible in a cottage which had been rotting for the last
ten years and upon which they had been working for
months. He had wanted to impress their London client
Mr Robert Escrick.

'I have worked down here, employed with this Cornish
firm for two years now and I have enjoyed my work; but
there is a problem with the natives . . . they're . . .'

'Yes?'

'They're, let's say, not like other people. They're a
people on their own; well, they're proud of it. You've just
got to get the . . . the *hang* of it.'

'You put village idiots in bolted bathrooms and missing front door keys in that category, do you? I've just got to get the hang of it?'

'It sounds a bit silly when you put it like that, sir. I really mean . . . you never know . . . quite . . . how things are going to turn out,' was as far as Jack Wither was prepared to go. They left it at that. But Jack said that he had seen the girl Mr Escrick meant, on the shore; she was some distance from Carrioth when she was on the beach down below here, but he was told she was a beach-comber and she picked up shells for a hobby; an expert in shell work, they told him, so she could not be that bad in the idiot line. She only looked unusual, and he ended with the slight joke that there were lots of village idiots about these days, there was one in the village the firm was in, too.

'And I don't mind telling you that there's quite a bit of activity along this stretch of shore.'

'What sort of activity?'

'I don't know for certain, my men never appear to understand what I'm talking about if I mention it, so I just don't. You see . . . on my rounds I try to turn up at every building site of ours once every day and there've been times I've arrived so late that the men have gone home, or just about to go; often it's been nearly dark and I've had to use my torch to see what they've done in a day, this last winter. I've seen lights down there, on the shore and among the rocks; I've not heard voices because they probably keep as quiet as they can; in any case, in the winter months there's the roar of the sea which would drown any noise at all.'

'Smuggling?'

He nodded. 'I dare say.'

'What sort of stuff?'

'Anybody's guess. Could be dope.'

Robert laughed and Jack Wither looked as though he wondered what he was laughing at. In fact he was laugh-ing it off, laughing off the feeling he had of annoyance and irritation that there should be anybody at all bent on any activity whatever in his carefully sought-after retreat.

'Come on,' Robert said, 'we'll go round the shack, stone by stone.' He realized that his steak would have to be for tea; in his new circumstances he would have to adjust himself to the plebeian feast of High Tea.

As they progressed he became pleased with what Jack Wither had done; he had interpreted Robert's wishes exactly, appreciating the mood which Robert wished his house to have. He had chosen exactly the right type of wood for the built-in furniture; naturally Robert had seen samples but now that it was all in place the effect was admirable. The Aga cooker sat smugly in its aperture where the old range had stood, and the kitchen cupboards and dresser around it; then, at the other end of the room was the great fireplace with logs piled against the wall beside. Along the south-facing wall on the sea side were the four original windows with the new shutters made in imitation of the old ones which for years had been left banging themselves to pieces in the glassless window-panes. There were bookshelves up to waist-high along the whole empty stone unplastered back wall and Robert had mixed feelings about these. The books he had brought would fill a few shelves perhaps, while the number of books he possessed would more than fill the lot. He would not be able to deal with that problem till he had written to Angela.

When planning his solitary retirement he had written to Angela some twenty times, a long explanatory letter which he carefully put away to think over, and after the lapse of a week or two, a new mood would come upon him and he would write another, a different kind of letter, tearing the rejected draft up and burning it when there was a fire in his study; otherwise carrying the bits round in his pocket until he was able to dispose of them in his office. The letter was still unwritten but he had plenty of time because Angela would be another few weeks in Sardinia.

Even the thought of writing to Angela unnerved him and made him absent-minded until the thought had

passed over; so he and Jack Wither arrived at the bathroom before he became alert again and concentrated on
the job in hand.

'. . . and you see I feel we should congratulate ourselves
about this,' Wither was saying proudly. 'It's at the back of
the house and never gets the sun and it would have been
dark with only that tiny window . . . as it is, you'll find all
your visitors will exclaim with delight at these glass roof
blocks.'

Robert had to laugh, these last two days were so unreal
his laughter spurted out partly nervously and partly in
great amusement at his own predicament.

'It's like a little cool, dripping green cave, if you left the
spray dripping,' and Wither stood on the bathroom stool
and grappled with the spray which, in fact, did have a
permanent drip. 'All the same,' he said ruefully, 'I'll have
to have that seen to.'

The roof blocks were discussed, and Jack Wither
declared them to be thicker than a normal brick when
they had in turn climbed the ladder which had been left
for the purpose and discussed the unlikelihood of any of
the blocks blowing off, even though the situation was
prone to gigantic storms. The inspection being now
virtually over, Robert could not but resort to an appraisal
which came very close to a small speech which he auto-
matically gave, to Jack Wither's great pleasure and his
own self-deprecation, because it was automatic and done
without a thought.

So Wither climbed into his car; there was still something . . . he had a friend who was a garden-planner and
had good experience in making storm-torn land into
presentable gardens.

'No,' Robert said firmly, 'absolutely not. I do not want
a garden!'

He had one; it was thrown open from time to time for
the District Nurse and Robert had always to be present,
stalking about his property and feeling somehow guilty,
being nice to people whose names he could never remember: 'Ah, you're here! How delightful of you to come . . .'

Never, never again. Whatever grew round his new home called Zoygate, it could continue to grow, and grow over the bare patches the builders had caused, right up to the walls; and never a lawn-mower would touch it.

'Yes, yes, I see the point . . .' Jack Wither started up his car.

'Oh, and if you hear anything about that shell girl Biddy Hallow in the course of your rounds, you'll tell me, won't you? And remember about the missing key!'

He waved him away. It was, in fact, five past three.

He snatched potatoes out of his basket, found the machine tool he had invented for peeling them, and stooped only a very little over the sink because it had been set in especially high to accommodate his six feet three. In half an hour he was sitting down on the bench at his splendid table and eating his meal, with *The Times* propped up against the wine bottle.

The twisted metal dolphin knocker outside the oak door was banged very loud and clear.

CHAPTER III

IT WAS two policemen in flat hats. Politeness overflowed.

'Good day, Officers!'

'Mr Robert . . . er . . . Escrick?'

He nodded.

'We would like a word with you, sir.'

'Certainly, but I have been held up this morning and have just prepared my luncheon; would you be kind enough to sit in your car till I have finished?'

'Certainly, sir.'

Robert hurried into his bedroom where he felt in the inside pocket of his town jacket where, sure enough, was the slim little case in which he kept his driving licence. He had not opened it for years but he trusted his secretary who always asked him for it on the relevant date. It was up-to-date and spotlessly clean as to endorsements, but as

he took it back to the table and finished his lunch he
cursed himself for the speed at which he had driven down
on the motorway. If the police could not anything like
catch up with him, they could easily telephone his number to places ahead. His feeling of release had been so
acute that he had behaved like some wild thing in the
jungle rather than the sober businessman he was forty-
eight hours ago.

But how the hell was he going to get out of this? . . . his
licence was still in the name of Cravenhead. It would be
far the best thing to incur a fine, keeping his licence out
of sight and saying it had disappeared, it must be lost. He
looked thoughtfully at the wine bottle behind *The Times*
on the table and decided to offer them each a tumbler of
wine if they were decent about the licence.

'Come in, Officers,' he cried jovially, welcoming them
with wide-open door. Very soberly they entered, neither
of them was Sergeant Crum, and sat on one of the
benches beside the table putting their hats on the table in
front of them; one of them took out a handful of forms
and taking up the top one he tucked a ballpoint pen
behind his ear: 'Your visit to the police this morning, sir,
with this village girl, what's her name . . . Biddy Hallow.'
He referred to the form he was holding, and upon which
Robert's eye was fixed because among other talents he
had the unimportant one of being able to read upside
down, and in handwriting beside the printed word, along
the dotted line he could see one four-letter word *rape*
standing out like a beacon light.

'I believe you took this girl to the police station in
Carrioth?'

'Yes.'

'Because you said you had found her in your bathroom,
she had locked – er – bolted herself in.'

Robert hated the way he put it: '*You said.*' But he
replied, 'Yes.'

'Well, sir, may we have your account of it?'

'Why? There was nothing in it. A girl I believe to be
slightly mentally defective . . . she can't speak above a

mumble . . . she wanders about the place, doesn't she? Unfortunately the builders, who have been here for months, were packing up over this last week, knowing I would be here yesterday. It seems they omitted to lock the front door before leaving. I say front door but there is, in fact, only one entrance door; I have had a visit from the architect who had the job in hand and he is going to make enquiries about it. The key is missing altogether, in fact.' He paused, he felt he was talking too much. He should dismiss them curtly. There was a tiresome long interval as though they were waiting for more.

They were.

Robert continued: 'I arrived very late, I'd driven from London, couldn't open the bathroom door. Left it a bit . . . tried again, heard moaning . . . woman's voice, faint . . . past midnight; I tried again . . .'

'What time would that be, sir?'

Hell, what did it matter?

'I didn't actually look at my watch. About midnight; anyway, it was dark . . . I have no electricity . . . I used candles . . . no telephone . . .'

That might have been a crime in itself; they exchanged shocked glances with one another at this significant slant to the situation.

'And then, sir?'

'Well . . . I just left things as they were.'

'You went to bed?'

'Yes.'

They seemed flabbergasted. Some explanation was imperative.

'I don't know this country, this district, this part of the world *at all*. I have come to live here because I liked it when I came over from Penzance some years ago.' He did not say how many. 'I knew of the existence of the village of Carrioth because I came through it on the way here.'

'Did you make any attempt to get the girl out of the bathroom?'

He was not going to make excuses. He said firmly: 'No,

I certainly did not! I had no tools for the job.' He
thought: First lie, I *had* my tool-box.

'Then how did you get her out?'

'I didn't *get* her out, I *let* her out.'

'You *let* her out?'

This was getting monstrous.

'I mean, she let herself out. I knew she must be in a
feeble state. She may have been drunk for all I know. In
the morning I simply talked to her kindly through the
closed door . . . she didn't speak a word.'

'Kindly?'

'I talked gently through the door. I had to raise my
voice a bit, of course, to make her hear. I just wanted her
to be assured that she must work the bolt out, if it was
stiff; work it gently out and open the door, I told her.
Now look here, Officer, I feel as though I have barely
arrived, I don't know my way around, I have scarcely
unpacked. Can't we just . . .' he gestured vaguely.

'I quite sympathize with you, sir,' the one who was
doing the talking said, 'but there's an old grandmother in
the village kicking up a real old shindy. She got the
doctor in within a few minutes, she's cook at the Parsonage,
and they couldn't even wait for an ambulance . . the
doctor took her off to hospital and she was . . . er . . . yes
. . . they coped with her, that is.' He did not seem to be
able to bring out what he was trying to say but he was
aware that Robert had had more than enough and
wished they would go. They both got up and the spokesman let the elastic snap back over his bundle of paper.

'You gave her breakfast, perhaps?'

'The girl was very weak, she could barely walk, I
threw her . . . I mean I put her down on my bed and went
to warm up some coffee and make toast. I gave her some.
She was whimpering, groaning all the time.'

As this talk was going on they were moving towards the
door, thus Robert became more relaxed and communicative. 'There was no question of chatting to her, or
trying to make friends or anything.' Robert thrust his
hands into his pockets. 'Rather extraordinary, don't you

think? Queer beginning to my first night in my new home,
I must say. Suppose I hadn't come down last night; now
the building job is finished, they've been working on it
for months, there'd be no one here today or tomorrow,
and if there had been, how would they know what was
going on, girl locking herself in, getting weaker and
weaker? . . . She might well have died!'

'Quite so, quite so.' The detective was thinking hard,
he could almost leave now without saying what he had
come to say. In desperation he looked at his partner in
this sickening assignation and this one did not put his
hat back on his head as the other had done when he
moved outside the door; he stood looking at him steadily,
obviously waiting for something.

'Well, you've been quite helpful, sir, thank you. If there
is anything else that comes to your mind, you will let me
know?'

Jovial again now that they were leaving, Robert said
that he certainly would not brood over the event; it made
him rather cross and slightly sick.

Oh well! If he was going to be like that, the policeman
would make him slightly sicker!

'You see, sir, the hospital found she had been criminally
assaulted!'

Robert felt dizzy with shock, as though his normally
flowing blood had halted, but he had had over the years
his quota of shocks, he had learned to cope with it.

He left his hands in his pockets and said casually: 'Oh
really! Then you've got problems coming to you, ha
ha!'

Non-comprehension abounded.

'When is a rape not a rape? It's got their Lordships
thinking!'

'Their Lordships?'

'The Law Lords.' Did they have newspapers down here
in this land's bitter end? Robert wished he had not said
what he said. Slowly and kindly and in as few words as
possible, he explained to what he had been referring: this
matter of rape being brought out into the open ground of

what was called the permissive society. The argument
being whether a woman, however much she might be
kicking and screaming, might not be thoroughly enjoying
her predicament. He said this as they walked towards
their Panda car and he felt that when they drove out of
sight, they would be giggling together. This feeling, however, was soon dissipated when the spokesman, sliding
open his window as he pressed the starter, thanked him
for the time he had given them and added, as he drove off:
'We'll be seeing you!'

CHAPTER IV

THERE HAD BEEN no question of offering them wine but
Robert now poured some for himself.

They would be back, of course; the girl would have to
tell her story again and probably again, but could she
talk? Was it only the grandmother who talked – and
talked? If she could, all might be well as soon as she
recovered from shock. She could bear him no malice
because he had done nothing; she was no doubt surprised
that outside the door was an elderly gentleman giving her
instructions about the sliding back of the bolt. She had
locked herself in because she was frightened by someone
who was not he. If she could talk she might be able to
gabble out a story of sorts and it might be a pack of lies or
it might not. If, on the other hand, she could not talk he
could hardly be accused upon such a really monstrous
lack of evidence.

She could, of course, be asked to identify the man of
whom she was afraid: is this he? And she might, in sheer
idiocy, nod her head. But how much would the evidence
of an obvious idiot count? When is an idiot not an idiot?

It was clear that he must find out whether or not the
builders were actually on the site, clearing up, the
previous day or the day before that. It was unlikely in the
extreme that the purchaser and new occupier of the

coastguard's cottage would, within the first few hours of his arrival at his newly restored property, make his first action a rape of the village idiot.

No, it was hardly that which he found worrying; it was the reporters in the local papers and what they would try to find out about him, Robert Cravenhead, *or* Robert Escrick. He had had quite a turn on looking at his driving licence in the name of Cravenhead. It was that sort of careless lack of concentration that would let him down.

Well, in the meantime, there was a great deal to be done in the way of tidying up and one of the blessings to hand was that he had no telephone . . .

He spent the rest of this first day exactly as he had planned. When everything was tidy he went for a long walk with Banjo on the beach; joyful because Banjo had so rightly decided to come away with him.

It was a shapeless coastline, rough and difficult because in places the incoming tide did not reach the cliff foot and in others it flooded right up beneath the cliff, smashing against the rocks at the cliff foot and pouring into the many caves. If, indeed, as the architect had said, the coast was used for smuggling it was the ideal district. And, furthermore, the five-mile stretch to right and left below Zoygate was far too difficult and dangerous for family cricket, bathing and simply lying in the sun, but perfection for an ageing businessman endeavouring to recover from the scars of forty years building up a business which had been forced upon him by inheritance.

With a watching eye on the tide, he had as long a walk as was possible, then came back along the cliff top and when he and Banjo got home they felt marvellous; he drank wine, ate bread and cheese and listened to Bach, and slept the sleep of one who believes that he has not slept for years.

Next morning the sky seemed to be pressed to the windows when he opened the shutters and there was a mindless mourning sound which rose and fell with monotonous moaning. An excellent time to write to Angela.

As a start he took out the draft of the letter he had written to his elder son who was now managing director of what had formerly been Cravenhead's.

May 20th

My dear Thomas,
I know quite well that you have, for the past year, suspected that there was, let us say, something in the air with regard to my retirement and I am grateful to you for letting things take their course without comment. Let us say that I am taking a 'sabbatical' like the legendary Jewish river that flowed every day except Sunday, or perhaps I should put it, I feel like one of the debtors and Israelite slaves that they released once every seven years. For reasons which you will understand I have been obliged to do this in absolute secrecy. But I trust you to make light of it to the world we live in; you may call it a sabbatical, if you like, for reasons which I find I cannot possibly explain; I have to keep it a secret. As you well know, the money situation has been entirely dealt with, as though I were dead, so there will be no question of my being dead because that would involve *being dead* which I would prefer not to do yet. But I have been salting away enough to live on comfortably, for ten years, in a bank which I shall never divulge, and not under the name of Cravenhead. They will let you know if and when I am dead.

Don't worry too much about the drop in home market orders, and the new export orders falling 5% as well; bear in mind that the order books are still astronomically high.

I shall continue to love you and Piers and to be proud of you, as I have always done. I never really deserved to be father to either of you.

But I still am
Your Father

There were many corrections but he had carefully copied the final draft and posted it on his way to the

Annual General Meeting in the letter-box at the post office in Threadneedle Street, and without any address for himself inside.

Then, once again, after all the attempts he had made to write a letter to his wife, he wrote:

My very dear Angela,

I am going to hurt you very much indeed. I am aware that I am being bitterly selfish but I am also aware that you can stand up to it. You may say that I have gone away for a long rest, which will be absolutely true, and you may say anything else you like about where I have gone; whatever suits you best. To your best friends you may even say that I have gone with another woman, if you like, but it won't be true.

The miserable truth is that I do not love you any more, though you have been to me the most marvellous wife that any man could wish for. The truly agonizing thing is that I do not know why this is so. I may be going mad.

Robert

He put the draft of the letter to his son back into his case and he left the letter to his wife on the table with a fresh sheet of quarto ready to copy it out. As he pottered about he thought over the letter and was not satisfied; it was about the twenty-first he had drafted and he considered that he had never yet hit off the moods, chosen the right words, or written the exact truth. Nor had he been able to decide where and how he should post it. Should he send it to his new bank and ask them to post it? He would not dare. He went through a long list of his personal business friends whom he could ask to post it, but every time he did so he disliked the idea more. He had thought of writing to friends all over the world asking them to post the letter to Angela, but that seemed a most deceitful thing to do. He thought of taking the fast early morning train to London and posting the letter from Paddington, but that seemed to be the trickiest idea of the lot; if he left it too

long he would be certain to meet his wife on Paddington
station, since she often travelled into Dorset to see her
mother, or she might have returned early when it was
reported to her that he was gone.

And lastly, he had quite seriously contemplated posting
it by pigeon post but gave this up as being the idea of an
idiotic boy scout and he would not know how to set about
it.

He tore the letter across and across and threw it to the
back of the fire; he watched it burn.

He stood outside in the damp fog, he could not see the
sea below but he could hear its gentle *shush* and not
another sound apart from the fog horn; not a car or a
lorry or an aeroplane or a tree-cutting saw, or a plough or
any other thing; this was what he had come for, why he
was here and he rejoiced.

But there is a limit to the amount of time you can
spend simply standing and rejoicing in a thick sea-mist,
being reminded of the sound of your mother's skirts as she
shushed in to say good night to you as a little boy, before she
went out to a ball.

Yesterday morning in the village of Carrioth he had
bought food for himself and Banjo but not enough for more
than one day. He would have enjoyed going into the local
inn, called the Shaven Crown, for the first time, and he
caught a glimpse, round the corner and down a little
street, of the sort of small harbour he had hoped to see,
but under the uncomfortable circumstances he resisted.

And he could not face Carrioth again today after
yesterday's experience, with everyone staring at him as
though he had arrived from Mars. It seemed that planning to build a new life for oneself, quite alone in a
remote place, needed as much care and thought as a
position at the top of a machine tool firm. He had to
remind himself that it was not a householder who had
occupied this building he had acquired but a coastguard, a
servant of the Admiralty, and he tried to think what the
day in the life of this coastguard would be like. Did he
have no cabbage patch at all? Was there a rota so that

one chap would take over from another weekly daily or
monthly? And how did it come that there was running
water? Did he live alone or was there someone else with
him? Could he be a coastguard *and* a householder with a
wife and kids? If so, how did the kids get to school, and
how did the wife do her shopping, three miles from
Carrioth counting the track from the cottage to the road?

Or did the coastguard live on fish and if so what sort of
fish; did he have a boat?

And if he was going to live the life of a coastguard how
was he going to tackle the gigantic list of reading he had
planned to do? Impatiently he gave up his thinking which
now amounted to worry; he locked the door and put
Banjo on guard. He climbed into the Range Rover.

Banjo would never allow him to go out for a walk or
any kind of fun without him, but he understood completely that it was not for him when the master got into a
car. Not counting the day before yesterday when the
master was climbing into a car with finality, and must
certainly take him, of course. So now Robert told Banjo
that he was on guard and that he, Robert, would be
back soon with lots of lovely grub including bones, and
drove away. He did not look at the map; he took the
road beyond where he turned off to Zoygate; he knew
there were villages galore and he wanted to pick out one
he liked and one which was not too small, and he had to
drive nine miles till he found one which would do.

Some weeks ago he had had sent down a small refriger-
ator for campers for which twelve watts of electricity,
the cigarette lighter in the car even, would be enough, or
Calor gas, so the first thing he did, groping round this
strange little foggy village, was to find a shop which sold
small Calor gas cylinders and this he did. He also asked
where the fish shop was and, trying to conceal his amusement at the question, the shopkeeper hurried to the door
and pointed down the street.

'Down that alley,' he said.

Robert saw no shop down the alley but he emerged on
to hard dirty sand on which an upturned boat stood with

baskets of fish quite obviously caught very recently lined
up in front; herrings, mackerel, (75p at Harrod's, 5p here
on the sands), and three restless grey lobsters. He left the
lobsters because he had no pan big enough for one, but he
bought herrings and mackerel which he would smoke
in the small smoking oven which one of his sons had
brought home from Sweden for his father.

Back in the sleepy main street he saw a small shop
which turned out to be a grocer's, remarkably well
stocked, where he bought tinned things; two large card-
board boxes were carried out for him, and he bought meat
and bones for Banjo in the shop which was the other half
of the grocer's. Banjo was not fussy about fresh meat, so
long as there was enough; if by any remote chance there
was too much, he would bury it and bring it up after a
carefully calculated length of time so that it was in a
condition that he liked, with the adequate amount of
living maggots as roughage.

He bought all the macaroni they had left in the shop
and he had a sack of potatoes carried out, and he bought
a tin-opener that could be fixed to the wall. He spent a
good hour over all this, then drove home through the fog,
making careful note of the road so that he would find it
again when the fog had cleared.

When he got back he was charmed with the scene that
met his eyes. Banjo was in fact really on guard, sitting in
that particular way he had which said: You're not
passing me, whatever else you may choose to do.

At first glance they looked like two schoolboys sitting
on a bright purple Honda motor-cycle and Banjo was
practically standing over them so that they should not go
a step further. On second thoughts the one on the carrier
was undoubtedly the elder, and when Robert had called
Banjo off and they both detached themselves from the
machine, Robert could not help but laugh.

Both now took off their helmets.

'How old are you?' Robert asked the younger. The
youth had a head of blond curls, like the boy in the
famous picture 'Bubbles'; physically he looked tough

enough but he had an absurdly baby-face. He did not answer immediately but the other spoke for him: 'He's just turned seventeen and passed his test for a motor-cycle under 250 cc. You should have seen him trying to throw his L-plates over the cliff in a strong wind!' He laughed. 'A comic kid but he can work when he wants, can Billy Bacup. He's a good boy, aren't you, Billy?'

'And you?'

'Fred Bedfont. I'm twenty-four. Worked for Brown & Bright ten years since I was a kid like 'im.'

His jeans were covered with a pale mud-dust, his boots splashed with the same pale dry mud, the laces gone and the toes upturned; a figure similar to some he had seen in the village of Carrioth. Pale Cornish earth.

Fred Bedfont was communicative; they had been sent to adjust the dripping spray in the bathroom and take the bolt off the bathroom door. Mr Wither was looking for a different type of bathroom door fixture, he'd come along and see if it would suit when he found one he liked.

'Are you a plumber or a carpenter?'

'Both; I bin working on this site since work started and so has Billy, here. Between us one of us has lost the key, the last day we was here, Tuesday. Mr Wither said to tell you and we're very sorry. Mr Wither says he's getting you a replacement.'

Robert looked at Billy and Billy looked boldly back at Robert, his face a blank. 'Never mind,' Robert said. 'Don't do it again!'

They were working in the bathroom for about half an hour and then Robert was asked to look at what they had done and see if it was OK. This he did, then watched them put their tools away in preparation to leave.

'Is it safe, you two, jammed on that machine?'

'No, it ain't,' Fred Bedfont said vigorously, 'it's not safe, sir. But this kid here, he's one of those economical types he calls himself, I can't hardly pronounce it, stingy, I'd call it. I bin taking him to work in my car most days, so there's times he's got to bring me and it's twelve miles, where we live.'

Bedfont was gently chaffing Billy but the boy seemed to take it all right. 'He's saving up, sir,' Bedfont went on as he pulled his helmet on and fastened the strap. 'He's saving up for the good life. That's what makes him work.'

'Is that so!' Robert changed the subject. 'What do you know about this girl Biddy Hallow, locking herself up in the bathroom?'

'Nothing, sir. We seen her around. A beachcomber, they call her, but my guess is she's only half there.'

'Did you see her recently?'

Both of them said no, and Fred went on to say they saw her last week, they couldn't remember what day, she was wandering about. The foreman was here and shouted her off.

'What day were you last here?'

They exchanged glances; what day was it?

'Tuesday we finished up,' Fred said thoughtfully.

'I was here on Wednesday night. Had she been wandering about?'

'She didn't come near the house, sir. The foreman saw to that; she made him mad-angry coming at all. He threatened her!'

'Threatened her?'

'Told her to piss off, sorry, sir. Wouldn't have her near. We bin here months, it was only the last two weeks she came further away from the village she lives in, over there. The weather was better, see? She wouldn't have known anything was going on here at Zoygate if she hadn't gone further than she ever goes, so they say. Warm sun, sea you can paddle in . . . that's what brought her out and once she saw us . . . well, she was curious, like. The foreman called her a damn nuisance.'

The kid now put in a few words, much to his senior's disapproval: 'It's all over the district, Biddy Hallow from Carrioth got locked up . . .' He croaked rather than spoke since his voice had barely broken.

'You get on with it, Billy, it's not for you to speak to the gentleman,' Fred Bedfont snapped.

If Robert had heard correctly the district had got it

wrong. Biddy Hallow had not 'got locked up'; she had locked herself up. However, he said nothing, he had yet to learn that in these outlying country districts local news passing rapidly from mouth to mouth became more and more distorted and fanciful. For the moment he simply wondered what else the gossipers knew, or thought they knew.

With much revving up, the purple, overloaded machine topped with the two bobbing white helmets snarled off, and after they had left there were no further visitors for nearly a week and the visit remained in Robert's mind as assurance that there were still other people than himself in the world.

The fog seemed to have come to stay, though often it gave signs of clearing because it was not static but blew hither and thither in all directions as though it were about to clear but could not decide. More fog wafted up gently in a non-existent wind.

Robert was in the strange condition of being absolutely alone for more than a few hours for the first time in his life. It had become a habit with him to wish to be alone, so much so that, finding himself really alone, he became slightly self-conscious and stiff with himself and Banjo, as one might in the constant presence of people he had never met before. He enjoyed the deep sleep, the records he had bought, some of which he had not yet heard; he enjoyed the herrings fried in oatmeal and egg coating, the smoked mackerel and his self-baked bread. He enjoyed banking up the fire with damp logs and hearing them gently hissing as they dried out. He unloaded the three packing cases of books which he had been collecting in his office for this very purpose for years, to the surprise of his secretary who commented from time to time. There were diaries and autobiographies which had been published over the past ten years and which he had never had time to read.

He had not been allowed to build a garage, so he had parked the Range Rover close to the back wall, out of sight, and for a week he took only short strolls through the

fog with Banjo because he was well aware that his sense of
locality was indifferent and there was a real chance that
he might not be able to find his way back to his cottage if
he strayed too far. However, the distant fog horn was a
comfort, surprisingly so, in fact.

It was not a gloriously happy week but neither was it
an unhappy one. It was a week of this slightly depressing
self-awareness. He began to wish the postman would call,
but of course he didn't. He wished, too, that a milkman
would come; that, too, would clearly not happen and he
had to cut down coffee-drinking since too much black
coffee was a bad thing, merely sharpening one's aware-
ness.

The main road from which one turned down to Zoygate
was marked on the map, but only very frailly as it was
second-class; several times he walked the track up to the
road with Banjo and simply stood waiting for something
to pass. He hoped a milk van of some kind might appear.
Cars and other vehicles did pass but on average of one
every five minutes and no driver paid the least attention
to the tall good-looking figure apparently waiting for
someone as he stood with his dog.

He thought of the many times he had cast *The Times*
away, angry with the bad news it always seemed to bear,
but now he was shocked to find himself actually wishing
for it.

He could judge just how far the edge of his piece of
land was from his cottage and he often strolled to this edge
and looked out into nothingness. This bit of cliff here at
Zoygate was not high and barely deserved the description;
it was neither sheer nor dangerous, there was only a short
sandy path winding down to the beach and nobody would
be killed if they managed to fall because the edge was not
defined; further along, the cliff rose sharply to some height
with exact limits as to edge, so anybody so inclined could
throw themselves down spectacularly whether the tide
was in or out. So this seventh day (and what day in the
week was it by the way?) he simply squatted on his own
'cliff top' with his arms round his legs and listened to the

gentle soughing below.

He could hear an accordion. Surely not! This must be the start of the hallucinations . . . no, he really did hear an accordion. One of his boys had had one, years and years ago when he was at his prep school. He had bought it from another boy who professed to have tired of this dated musical instrument. Piers had taken the thing over, he remembered, as Thomas had failed to be able to play it at all. Piers played it quite well until, of course, the Beatles had produced a new kind of sound and the accordion had been thrown into an attic; he had seen it only the other day when he had been looking for his old pair of boots. There was a trace of excitement in the way Robert stood up as though about to bound down the sandy track and investigate in a Dr Livingstone I presume frame of mind.

How simple can you get when you have lived as yet only a week entirely alone? At the sound of nearby mankind he was becoming suddenly excited. He made himself faintly sick. Calling Banjo, he stamped back to the cottage and put on some Vivaldi.

Nevertheless, he heard the sound of the accordion again, and even again.

And then two mornings later a great light shone through the cracks in his bedroom shutters; he jumped up, flung them open and saw that the fog had gone and blazing sunshine flooded the outdoor scene. His windows faced south and the sun was slanting across them from the east and he experienced this happiness that he had felt so few, few times, when he was here before. There, out on the sea, was the tiny red sail of a boat of sorts. This very day he and Banjo would explore. And that was the day he met Roundstone and nothing was ever the same again.

CHAPTER V

HE WAS WALKING about as he played and whether he saw Robert and Banjo or not, he did not appear to do so. He was a thin man, neither tall nor short, and even at a distance he had the appearance of a predatory bird with this great beak, which turned out to be a nose, the bridge of which was like fine polished mahogany. The sea-shore with the tide out was exactly the right place in which to observe him for the first time; the tide was at its lowest and calmest, and as he walked barefoot along its very edge his form was reflected in the ebbing water; his pale blue jeans were rolled up to above his knees and he wore, by accident or design, a fisherman's windcheater of the same colour.

The relief that Robert felt that there were still people in the world caused him to demonstrate how little he cared, and he threw stones for Banjo to retrieve, which, though a retriever by name, Banjo never did. He ran, he located the stone, he sniffed it, returned laughing to his master, appreciating the joke. This farce was carried out till they were two or three hundred yards from the other human being, then Robert turned and retraced his steps very slowly; far be it for him to appear to be seeking company on the shore. He was wearing espadrilles so he was higher up, on the dry hard sand.

The accordionist was now coming in his direction and as he drew level they were some fifty yards apart. If there had been any life in this morning's tide his voice could not have been heard, but this morning it was so mild and still that his voice carried: 'Hallo! Who are *you*?'

Perversely, Robert had to see his face close up before he answered and he spent a quarter of a minute looking before he answered: 'Escrick.' This slowness in answering a sudden question was an idiosyncrasy of Robert's that unnerved many people.

'Roundstone,' the other returned as he struggled to pull the too-short strap of the accordion over his head. 'Beach-comber. Age forty-three.'

'And an Irishman,' Robert added.

'That's right, how did you guess?' the other said sarcastically. 'Still an' all, it's not a strong accent, is it?'

'Merely a tinge,' Robert reassured him, 'but unmistak-able.'

'As a matter of fact, you must be the feller who has bought up the old coastguard station at Zoygate,' and he pointed a finger at it. 'Up there. I've been up there many a time and oft, to see what was going on. You've been doing yourself well, have you not? The place used to be occupied by a diddicoi family and oh, my Lord!'

They were strolling side by side up the beach now. Robert waited for an explanation. 'Diddicoi?'

'A kind of rotten, bad quality gipsy . . . they played hell with us; we were right glad to see them go.'

'Were they here long?'

'Never for long at a time. They came . . . they went . . . and before you could say knife, there they were, back again, their rags spread about all over, squatting. Since your place was condemned there was no question of rent in a situation several miles from anywhere; it was derelict like thousands of bothies of that kind scattered about all over Cornwall, so they tell me. They spread their rags around the place, supposedly newly washed, but who could tell? It was anybody's guess and mine was they were signalling to enemy aircraft . . .' And he burst into wild laughter at his own joke. 'They have a camp up there beyond the new station at the top of the hill. The kind Council lets them stay as long as they want but it's powerful cold up there most of the year. Lord knows where they find to go in winter, but as I'm only a bicycle-driver, I've never located them in winter. Perhaps they follow the moles and rabbits, underground!'

'Where do you live, then?'

His boat was now lolling on the sand where the tide had

receded and left it stranded. He gestured with a hand. 'That's my boat,' he said unnecessarily.

It seemed it could be the little craft Robert saw from his windows, with red sails; it was mostly evident in the evenings, but now the red sails lay in a heap on the wet sand.

Robert stopped where the path started and turned to Roundstone: 'You'll know all about my pad, then? You wouldn't like to come and look, now it's finished?'

'I would, sure.'

Robert found himself wanting to show someone, even somebody who had seen it before. He had a modest pride in the place when he remembered what a ghastly ruin it had been. 'I've left the walls unplastered,' he explained as he almost hurried up the path. 'Do you know Jack Wither, the architect? I do admire that chap's know-how. He's quite talented. Curious to find someone with ideas in this land's end, what?'

He had arranged a drink tray, as he always had at home, and gave his guest a good strong whisky with the thought that it would loosen him up; so much, perhaps, that he would go so far as to tell Robert where he lived.

Roundstone admired Banjo and Robert explained that he was, in fact, bought with his brother as pedigree black labradors. The brother had been called Ben and he had been called Jo. Labradors, as he must know, grew very quickly and they were fully grown when he bought them, said to be five months old; *however*, they astonishingly grew longish hair and the family, shocked though they were, would not return them to the breeder because they were already so dearly loved; they called them 'our rough-haired labradors'. Then his younger son, who had a small country estate, begged to keep one and this one was left on his own; they couldn't decide whether to call him Ben or Jo, so he was called both and, of course, in time ... etc.

The whisky was having a visible effect. Though this had been the object in plying him with it, Robert was mildly surprised that it was having such a rapid effect. Roundstone sat opposite in the other rocking-chair, his back to the windows, talking. He changed the subject from himself and waved his glass approvingly. 'You've done well, man, very well. The stone walls . . . the bookshelves . . . that end the kitchen, this end the drawing-room . . .'

'Living-room!'

'The diddicois wouldn't know themselves!'

'The only trouble is, when I fry fish, which I'm always doing, or smoke it, which I do less often, the smell travels over here . . . however, I'll get used to it.'

'Bring your herrings down to the beach and fry them,' Roundstone cried cordially. 'Out in the open air they smell grand . . .'

Robert gave him another two fingers of what Roundstone called *the strong stuff*, filled the tumbler with ginger ale and just hit off a nice mood of confidence. It was he who broke up the session by standing up and saying: 'Well, I must get on with things,' which, alas, after he said it, he was not asked to specify. But he had to get Roundstone to go before his legs gave way.

As it turned out he had no trouble with him. First he said: 'Show me the rest,' and Robert said there was hardly any 'rest' but he flung open his bedroom and exhibited the wall-long built-in cupboard, the fixed bed with shelves on either side, the window-shutters.

The door to the bathroom . . .

'. . . and the toilet!' Roundstone banged the closed door with his hand.

'Shower and lavatory,' Robert said curtly.

'Oh . . . yes,' Roundstone agreed, mysteriously elongating his vowels.

'So that's it,' Robert returned hurriedly.

Outside, successfully, the visitor plucked Robert's sleeve. He jerked his head. 'Over here, come on.' He led him some hundred yards eastwards and Robert wondered what on earth he was up to. He was only getting them into a position from where, to Robert's surprise, the new coastguard station was visible, much higher up the cliff and hidden from view by a promontory between itself and

Zoygate, but very much there topping the cliff and not far away. It was a low grey building, merging with the surrounding grey crags, and there was a prominent flag-staff and a few out-buildings.

'I say new, but it's been built a good fifteen years now. We've been talking about your pad, you should see mine, only you're not going to today. No room for two, even standing up. It's a shepherd's shelter probably; if it was on the edge of a village they'd say it was the old village lock-up. I repaired it myself and I get it for free, working as odd job man at the station.' He stood at attention and banged his chest comically: 'I work for the Admiralty, I'll have you know, and I'll tell you another thing, that's the first whisky I've had for seven years!'

'Surely,' Robert exclaimed, 'your pay covers a tot of whisky now and then?'

'They pay me all right – ' He quickly changed the subject, clicking his fingers for Banjo.

The walk back to the footpath down the bank to the beach was carried out successfully, though his guest was slightly wobbly.

'Are you all right?' Robert asked, apparently with kind anxiety for his guest's welfare.

'Just a wee bit on the smokey side,' was the reply. 'It's too many years since I've tasted the strong stuff, and thanks.' He wandered off, accordion hanging from his shoulder, and Robert watched till he was safely out of sight. Then he returned to his living-room and poured out a whisky for himself; so far he had been drinking only ginger ale.

He thought about what his new neighbour had told him. It seemed quite clear that Roundstone had been born into money and had never really had to work for it; there was nothing the least navvy-like about him. His father had died when Roundstone was twenty-two, so he had said, and he had had to take over the business which was boat-building. He had not planned that kind of future for himself but there was no alternative, he had said; he had met a girl he wanted to marry . . . and that was that, he had said. There was a marvellous old foreman at the shop and he not only kept things going . . . or was it just the growth of the affluent society? . . . the business flourished, they sold their boats all over the world, including places like Malaysia and the Philippines, and latterly Kuwait, he had said. He too, had gone all over the world, collecting orders. It was all right for a bit but you got sick of it, he had opined. He had had to go off the drink entirely, he had said, and fluently.

All might have gone well if the foreman, God rest his soul, hadn't died of a heart attack . . . after that nothing went right. The whole thing broke up, went bust. And that would be the moment his wife and daughter left him, just walked out, he had said.

What he had said about 'the drink' was ambiguous because it was probable that it was the drink which caused the wife and daughter to 'walk out'. What he did not say was that he had had to 'take the pledge' to save himself from whisky. However, there was now good news about 'those two bitches'. The wife had a job as buyer for a London store and the daughter had married a business-man and was 'busy having babies in Brighton'.

Robert wanted very much to ask him, 'What do you do for money?' But he had done well enough; he had learned all that without having to give any information about himself in return. There was a warmth about the man which made Robert like him; there was also a weird lack of credibility, his life-story was too glib.

The next weeks went past without any event at all except lovely weather; unless you could call a visit from the Rating Office's officer an event. He came for informa-tion regarding rates and went away a disappointed man because there was no street lighting, no paving, no garage, no out-buildings (not even a log shed), no lane to be kept passable, no tap for watering the garden or cleaning the car, and no garden to water anyway.

Roundstone was there and Robert was pleased. Some-times he came in for a drink, sometimes they met on the shore sometimes they walked for miles and Robert learned nothing more about him; after that first outburst, he never mentioned his past life or his family. When he did not have his accordion with him he had a mouth organ, which he would take from his pocket and play from time to time.

Robert was neither happy nor unhappy, he was simply bewildered. Time and again he would settle to have a long careful look at himself but it was never a success. He went as far as admitting that he was a total extrovert; in all his fifty-eight years he had never taken a long close look at himself. What kind of thinking was it that caused him to believe he must leave his home and family and live totally alone, without letting anybody who knew him know where he was? How did this behaviour relate to an extrovert of his quality?

He came to the conclusion that he was one of those thinkers who think on two or more levels. He had met about three in his life; one at school. This boy was full of ideas, sudden ones; he would shout his instant ideas to all and sundry, and later one would find it was not at all what he thought and when closely questioned he would shrug it off with an: 'Oh, well, I expect I'm talking rot!'

Robert was aghast at the duration of time this thinking, so called, of his had lasted; he had been planning it for ten busy and successful years, during which the business had thrived and multiplied exceedingly. Here he was, shipwrecked yet with every comfort, a kind of latter-day Robinson Crusoe.

It was the writing of The Letter to Angela which was causing this unwelcome metamorphosis; he had planned that this had to be done by the end of the second week after his transplantation. So, shortly after his first meeting with Roundstone:

Dear Angela,
    You may have noticed my absence.

'No!' he cried, asking himself how cheap and nasty he

could get. He crumpled the plain writing paper and started again:

Dear Angela,

By now you will have realized that I have finally achieved the condition of life which I used to discuss with you, so long ago when we did discuss things together. I have everything for which I have been planning, marvellous surroundings, food, company and occupation, so you will realize that there is no need to worry, not that you ever have worried –

'No, no, no!' he cried out so vehemently that Banjo got up and came across from the warmth of the Aga to investigate.

There was just one thing by which he was not unduly worried and it was the fear that Angela might employ a private detective to try to discover his whereabouts. He was quite certain that he had left no clue at all and Angela might realize that she had the whole world in which to search; she was not one to waste money unduly.

On the other hand, she might not make the slightest attempt to find him; she might tell their friends that he had gone off on a long holiday, and as time went on this holiday could be extended indefinitely until the memory of Robert faded gradually.

Nobody had ever been so completely on his own, he decided, and nobody so very alone could do other than look himself in the face and wonder what sort of person he was; he would lose infinitely, he would shrivel mentally, he would decay visibly like a house from which the owners have gone and are not replaced.

He had the welfare of only himself and Banjo to consider and it would not do. What about the poor idiot Biddy Hallow? He should have called at her grandmother's cottage to enquire about her; it was too ridiculous that he should have completely ignored that unpleasant event. And having had a constructive thought, he must at once act upon it, since it was all too easy to fall into the decay he had envisaged.

His map showed him that if he wished to get to the village of Carrioth much the most pleasant way of going was along the shore – that is, so long as the tide was not in because it was impossible to see from the map whether the tide came right up to the cliffs or not. If it did, if it came flooding in and surging into the caves, as he knew it did in places he had already been to, he might quite well drown.

INDUSTRIALIST FOUND DROWNED. How dull that would be; what dark secret would it be assumed he took with him; what had caused his inability to face himself, or, facing himself, could not bear what he saw?

Leaving Banjo on guard, very apologetically, he took off his espadrilles and with a piece of string threaded through the back of the heels, he hung them round his neck. He could walk in bare feet along the hard sand indefinitely. The tide was on the turn and he realized that if he stayed any length of time in Carrioth the incoming tide would oblige him to walk back along the road. Three-quarters of the way was high cliffs and innumerable caves which it would take years to explore.

It was smugglers' territory, Free Traders they used to be called, and the coastguards would carry warrants for their arrest in the King's name; some of them evaded arrest for years before they were sent to the gibbet. In those days there was a great variety of contraband goods landed on these shores, now there was a much smaller variety: contraband people and opium mainly, and Roundstone told him there was a constant watch for oil slicks which had to be dissipated rather than exterminated.

'And what are you keeping watch for, with your little red sails?' Robert had asked him.

'I live on fish, I couldn't eat a piece of fish that hadn't come straight out of the Channel now. I've been at it for years, I can just about pull them out with my fingers.' And when Robert settled down to discuss choice of fish, he laughed and waved it aside, saying he took the first he saw. So long as it was fresh, he liked the lot.

The cliff top sloped down sharply to rocks, with sand-hills behind and finally the village of Carrioth, which he was now looking at from the shore and of which he could recognize nothing he had seen upon his first visit except the ugly pointed tower of the nonconformist-looking church. There was the church, so near there would be the Parsonage; he ought to pay a visit to the Parson, not with any intention of going to church but to enquire after his dotty parishioner with the vile grandmother who was the Parson's cook. The approach to the village was a narrow lane, and beyond Robert could see the tiny harbour.

Boats were lying about here and there and the sand underfoot became soft and slippery and none too clean. With the little church spire ahead of him he tramped off the shore and through the village, looking neither to left nor to right, in case he caught sight of an ugly look, as he had before.

The short damp approach, overgrown with seedy rhododendrons, was the way he must go, and not stroll carelessly to the kitchen entrance which branched off to the right. He hoped fervently the Parson was at home; otherwise, if he rang the front door bell it might be answered by the Hallow hag. And to his immense relief he found the front door wide open and the parson himself sitting on the front steps reading the parish magazine of a neighbouring church.

Without giving his introduction any thought Robert held out his hand and said: 'Robert Escrick, the new owner of Zoygate.' The little man looked over the top of his half-moon glasses, exclaiming suitably enough: 'Bless my soul!' and it was not easy to say whether he deliberately ignored Robert's outstretched hand or not.

The parson was confused and appeared flustered, none of his customers was so big and so confident-looking, spoke in such an important voice and wore dark glasses; if it had been St Paul himself he would probably have behaved exactly the same way. 'Oh, you want to see old

Mrs Hallow, I . . . I'll fetch her for you . . .' He scrambled up.

'Not at all, not at all, sir, I came to see you, if I may. Couldn't I sit down here on this bottom step? It's probably pleasantly warm.'

'Of course, of course. I expect you've called about poor Biddy. I believe it was at Zoygate . . . Zoygate, that is . . . yes, yes, of course . . . the new owner . . . well, well.'

For a half minute Robert allowed him to be embarrassed, to bluster and stammer and altogether let himself lose control of the situation, then recovered.

'Yes, Zoygate, where your local village idiot was reported to have been criminally assaulted,' he said crudely, causing the parson to shrivel even more uncomfortably. It was the sort of situation with which he was not familiar. 'Oh no, no! You must not refer to our Biddy as . . . that is, in such a way, such a manner. Indeed not!'

Robert ignored that, but said that as it happened to be in the bathroom of his new house that she was found, locked in by herself, and as he had been unable to get any explanation out of her, or indeed any intelligible words whatever, he could but refer to her as he had.

The strange little man screwed up his eyes and the parish magazine at the same time. 'She's not quite, no, she's not an idiot; poor Biddy has some sort of mental defect with which she was born. I baptized her myself, she is now thirty, and this condition of hers has never been identified; nobody has tried to identify it. She's quite happy as she is. Why, why . . . why bother to – to – to examine her and state what *kind* of dementia she suffers from? What good would it do?'

Robert simply stared and for understandable reasons did not help the poor stammering parson in the least. He sat on the bottom step looking remarkably at his ease, while the holy man sat on the top step, three up, and writhed with embarrassment.

He waffled on for some long time, giving out no more information, and Robert decided that he would learn nothing more unless he shocked more definitely. He said bluntly: 'I was told by the police that she was criminally assaulted, and there was quite a pointed implication of myself in their manner. I had been at my new house about ten minutes when I found her. I also found the front, in fact, the only entrance door unlocked and no key except the one I held myself, which had been sent me by the builders' architect. The girl Biddy had used a bolt in the bathroom.'

This was quite a successful move because the parson at last looked at him straight, and not askance. What sort of man is this? he seemed to be asking himself.

Robert continued: 'The whole idea that I had anything to do with it is absurd. I have been to Zoygate around half a dozen times since I decided to buy it, which was the first time I ever saw it. I have never been into this village until that day I brought in the girl I found in my bathroom, and yet I am convinced that the entire population believe I was the one who done it. Raped her, I mean.' At which the parson grimaced as violently as though he had caught his finger in his car door. It appeared he was enduring sheer agonized physical suffering.

'Don't any of you read the papers? Don't you know that you should all be keeping your heads over the subject of rape now? Haven't you read or heard what their Lordships the Law Lords have said? Where is this Land's End? Is it about three hundred and fifty miles from London, or is it out on its own in, say, mid-Pacific?'

The parson was scrambling to his feet now; he was fizzing gently with what Robert took for anger. He said: 'You surely don't expect me to preach a sermon on it, do you? Besides, down here at the Land's End, as you call it, we are not familiar with the crime you mention!'

'Oh, good for you!' Robert was ready to sit and discuss it at length, quoting the actual wording of the new resolution supporting the Sexual Offences (Amendment) Bill, but the parson was clearly trying to terminate this very unwelcome visit. Robert, taking the hint, unfolded what seemed the yards of himself and stood up. 'You are fortunate, Mr – er – in having a splendidly crime-free flock.'

The parson had a pursed little mouth and did not relax it at Robert's only semi-serious remark, meant to please.

'Crester is my name,' he snapped, then: 'You must realize that we are a village of some two thousand souls. The Hallow family, though nearly all are now dead, were known by everybody and Biddy's grandmother is my housekeeper. She has been deeply distressed by this – this affair. I personally do not for one moment believe that a newcomer to the village would – er – assault a young woman he meets within, as you say, minutes of his arrival. But the village is so – so – so indignant, there must be a culprit, you understand?'

'No. But never mind. Just let me have a word with old Mrs Hallow.'

'What for?'

'Not to apologize, if that's what is upsetting you. No, merely to express my regret that ... well ... that I found her granddaughter in my bathroom, locked in, and that I hope ... well, I suppose I shall have to say *hope* that she is none the worse ... or better now, if you'd rather?'

'I would strongly advise you ... no. She is exceedingly upset. I really don't know what would happen if you went into the kitchen to see her now.'

'You mean, she'd chuck a heavy dish at me, or something?'

Mr Crester looked exasperated. 'Mr Escrick, I do advise you to go. I – I – I shall think over what you have told me and I appreciate your visit.'

'And you'll tell them in church on Sunday in your sermon – what is it? Remind them about casting the first stone, or something.'

Robert's retreat was slow, steady and dignified; he only wished he had a drum to beat upon.

So back on the beach the best he could make of his enterprise was that he had paid attention and not just ignored the whole squalid little affair. He had spent about a quarter of an hour at the parsonage so the tide would not have made much progress; taking off his espadrilles he again hung them round his neck. He still had his dark glasses on and after he had gone a mile or so he took them off and rubbed them clean because he could see something some distance away but could not make out what it was. In his nervous state he thought it might be a drowned body, flung carelessly down by powerful waves, but today was so mild the tide was freewheeling gently in and would not have knocked over even a homeward-bound snail. As he approached he realized, too late, that it was none other than the redoubtable Biddy Hallow. She was lying on the hard sand, face downwards, and poking with a stick under a rock which hung over a small pool left by the tide. She rolled over on her back as though he had called her name as he approached.

He at once veered away, walking hurriedly seawards again, but she called him in a high piercing voice something that sounded like: 'Mister, Mister!' He had to stop and look back out of sheer mercy. How did she get up? She looked as though she was wearing seaweed but it was some kind of mini dress in remarkably poor condition and showed her long, skinny white legs, one of which seemed to be dragging behind. It struck him at once, though he knew nothing about it, that there was no malformation of her legs but that she preferred to walk that way, probably to draw attention to herself. Simply guesswork.

He stood still, out of sheer good manners, until she came up beside him and, smiling that chilly, knowing smile he had seen before, she stroked his arm. She had a flat fish-basket with six-inch sides hanging from her arm and she brought out a handful of shells, picking one out here and there and holding it up for him to see. Robert had never in his life been more bewildered. His flesh crawled as though he had a bat in his hair; he could not bring himself to touch her. He looked wildly round: the sand, the creeping sea, the cliffs, the scattered rocks and not a human being in sight, nor a vessel on the shimmering sea, not even a red sail to be seen.

Now she clutched one end of the silk scarf he wore knotted in the open neck of his shirt; he caught her icy, brittle wrist and tried to pull it away. It was rapidly developing into a struggle; he prised her off him and, taking both her shoulders in a firm grip, he held her at a distance.

'What were you doing in my house?' He waited and he had no doubt at all that she understood. 'I have a very fierce black dog at my house and if you come, he will rush at you and knock you down and you won't like that, will you? He is trained as a guard dog, and if I were not there to call him off, he might hurt you very badly, do you understand?'

She shook her head.

'You do understand, I know you do!' He let go of her and started to walk away hurriedly. He turned and looked back to where she stood like a crushed and dying wild flower that a child has manhandled, head hanging, legs all awry. 'Now remember,' he shouted, 'you have been warned!'

CHAPTER VI

ROUNDSTONE took a long pull on his glass and hiccoughed slightly. 'The *throuble* is . . .' Long pause while the wind and the rain threw what sounded like tiny pebbles against the windows.

'The trouble is,' Robert put in, 'that the more whisky you have the more Irish you become, so if you're trying to hide the fact that you're Irish you'd better cut it out.'

'Oh, you're the clever one! What was I saying? The trouble is that I was born in a font, at the church of St Agnes in Manchester. No, I'm pulling your leg, I'm inaccurate, I don't mean born so much as left.'

'Left?'

'Just put there by my father when I was, say, a week old.'

Robert looked puzzled.

'Oh, I know what you're thinking! You're thinking, how did he know it was his father. Well, I'll tell ye. Years later, years later I visited The Birthplace; the church of St Agnes in Manchester. It has a very fine font, I reckon the top's four feet high . . .' He looked questioningly at Robert who could not take that one.

'Couldn't have been,' Robert exclaimed.

'It has a very fine top, this font, you could go and see for yourself.'

'Wouldn't dream of it.'

'Well, when I was found in it, the lid was taken off and laid down beside the . . . the font.'

'It might have been better to have put back the lid on top of you where it belonged.'

Roundstone gave a long wheeze of laughter. 'Indeed, you're right! But the point I'm trying to make is that it must have been my father put me there because a woman could never have lifted that lid off, never. And can you see any man being so obliging as to bring another man's baby and put it in that font? Lifting off the lid to make a proper job of it?'

'Yes, I can. The man who made the baby might quite well have taken the task upon himself, but it seems to me more likely that the husband of the woman who was seduced by the man who wouldn't own the baby might have done so, if you insist that it was a man who done it. Why not a woman put the baby in the font?' (Guesswork again?)

Crestfallen, Roundstone said that he always believed his father had done that deed. He, Roundstone, had been wrapped in a warm shawl and laid inside the font from which the huge heavy lid had been lifted, by . . . yes, he could laugh but it meant a lot to him . . . *by loving hands* . . . b'gad.

The verger had found him because of the screams. The verger had carried him, early in the morning, to the community of sisters connected with the church of St Agnes in Manchester and they had taken him in and later they

told him they considered his age to be between three
weeks and a month when he was found and this was in
1932.

'So I set out on my life with three dozen or so mothers,
all Irish ladies, so that's where I get what you so sharply
discover, an Irish accent. But wait a minute – ' he raised
a warning finger – 'wait a minute . . . what fell out of the
shawl that was wrapped round that wee babe?'

'I've no idea,' Robert admitted coldly, 'what fell out
of the wrappings.' Nevertheless, he tried: 'A sovereign?'

'This!' he returned triumphantly, taking it out of his
pocket and holding it up: a small round stone.

'Which accounts for your name. And I was there at
Roundstone in Connemara with my father and two
brothers on a fishing holiday when I was a boy. Well,
well!'

'Did you go to Roundstone?'

'We passed through it.'

'What sort of place is it, like?'

'I can't remember it except that we were amused at the
name. But all Connemara . . . lovely. Just about as west as
you can get . . . Next stop, the Statue of Liberty.'

This amused Roundstone, who was easily amused, but
Robert was wondering why, since he himself must come
west to Land's End, he had not considered going to the
westernmost land's end, Connemara instead of Cornwall?

It was a wild evening but not cold, and the sea was
making a stimulating roar but without the vicious note
that could be heard when it really meant business. Where
was Roundstone's boat? He said it was hidden from sight
in a secret place: a cave which turned the corner at the
top, and ran a few yards to a dead end which was completely invisible from the shore. The tide only just reached
the bend and, of course, the boat could only be approached
when the tide was out, so it was more often than not left
lying on the beach in the summer, and in rough weather
alongside the coastguard station's little jetty.

'Really?' Robert said. 'You must show it me some
time.'

'Not I!' Roundstone chuckled. 'It's my turn now to laugh and not tell you what I'm laughing at.'

'If you must know,' Robert said, 'I was laughing at the thought of whether, as a baby of a month old, crying in a font in Manchester, your nose showed signs of turning out like it has.'

So Roundstone did find this funny, and when he had stopped laughing he said he would now walk home over the cliff top since the wind made riding a bicycle rough and the tide was full in tonight. This could not be less than the hundredth time he had done it, so Robert made no protest but offered him a big torch, because darkness had fallen during the recital of Roundstone's antecedents. Roundstone begged him to keep his torch for his own needs. But Robert argued that with all that whisky inside, Roundstone would walk back home along the cliff top only at very great risk since, *since,* Robert reminded him emphatically, he had told Robert that it was years since he had tasted the strong stuff.

'Did I really tell you that?'

'You did.'

'Ah well, you mustn't believe every word I say . . .' He clapped Robert on the shoulder and started to walk away, but looked back and cried: 'Next time you must tell me about yourself.'

'I will,' Robert shouted against the wind, 'I will indeed when I've had time to think something up!'

All his life Sir Robert Cravenhead had been the north-countryman he was born and he never tried or even contemplated being someone other than the craggy character he was, and never smooth and silky. Now, he was distinctly uneasy to discover, he found himself thinking: How shall I play this? Looking back to his interview with the fussy little parson, he realized that he had not given his own behaviour a thought, and when he left, he now remembered the parson would not 'be on his side'.

But what the hell?

The hell was, that peace to him meant peace of mind

and this he had never had because there had always been
something at the works to worry about. So he had spent
a lot of time and thought, not to forget money, in planning to have peace of mind and still he had not achieved
it. There was the encounter with the menace on the
beach, who had now come a long way from being the
amusing 'Twitty Woo' he had first thought her. It was
the solitariness of it that worried him. If she could talk –
and it appeared she might well be able to, or at least
communicate – she could accuse him of the direst
behaviour and he could not produce a single soul who
knew Robert Escrick and could vouchsafe for his
integrity.

His only hope lay in whether or not she made a habit
of this sort of thing, and if she was indeed thirty, there
was every possibility that this insane conduct of hers was
recurrent. So he sat rocking gently in his chair, reading
Almayer's Folly by Joseph Conrad which he had never had
time to read, yet not taking in a word but worrying about
whether the village idiot made a habit of importuning
men *or not*.

And through the pouring rain came the architect Jack
Wither, from Brown & Bright, the building firm, with the
final bill for the last of the work done on Zoygate. The
previous four accounts had been handed to him in this
manner on the occasions he had come down to inspect
progress and each time he had taken out his cheque-
book and paid at once, so there was nothing unusual in
the intent of his visit.

Once more they walked round discussing this and that.
Robert had no complaints and soon another type of lock
was to be fitted. Jack Wither asked if he was now satisfied
with the bathroom spray and Robert said yes, he was. He
went further to comment on the young chap who had
been sent to do the job. 'That golden-haired monstrosity
and the other called Fred you sent to do the lock gave me
the impression that they had done most of the work up
here themselves,' he said with amusement.

'Fred Bedfont is a gem,' Jack Wither said warmly.

'Billy Bacup was one of those who make a shocking start, then do very well. He's ambitious.'

'The one called Fred believes he did the cupboard himself.'

Jack Wither was amused now. 'He believes he did, so perhaps 'nuff said. He works twice as well as any of our workmen; he's keen, first on the job, and doesn't bother about dinner break or tea break if he happens to be interested in what he's doing, and he's as strong as one of these champion weightlifters there used to be in circuses and at fairs long ago.'

Smiling, they both sat down at the table and Robert took out his cheque-book and pen. 'I'm very satisfied,' he said as he pushed the cheque across.

'Thank you, sir.' Jack Wither folded it but when he looked up from tucking the cheque in his breast pocket his face was serious. 'You remember telling me that if I ever heard anything about the Biddy Hallow episode the day you came, I should tell you.'

'Yes?'

'I hate doing it, sir. You . . . newly arrived and settling in, it doesn't seem fair to . . . well, I have to say *upset* you. I know I'd be upset in similar circs.'

'There's a rumour going round that I raped Biddy Hallow?'

'*Rumour!* Nobody seems to be able to talk about anything else. Not at first, mind you . . . but you've been here, how long now? Five weeks? For the past week it's been raging. Everyone's asking everyone else if they've seen you. It's not only Carrioth, mark you, it's spread to the villages round, like. Blow me, it's like rabies. Anyone would think there'd never been a rape here since the Garden of Eden.' But he looked serious and worried.

'What I'm wondering, sir, is what the dickens you can do about it? What about getting a solicitor? You see, the fact that you've just arrived, out of the blue, no family, all alone . . . makes a bit of a story out of it. They're great ones for legend down here. They're out of it: terrible things happen elsewhere but never here, and now, at last, there's something to be going on with . . . blowing it up out of all proportion!'

He looked across the table questioningly, straight into Robert's face. Then he got up, saying he would be on his way, and Robert still said nothing but he got up too and showed him to the door. He did not say anything because he did not know what to say and this alarmed Jack Wither slightly. Just as he started up his car Robert shouted from his door, through the pouring rain, 'Thank you, thank you for telling me,' and stood in the open doorway until Wither had driven off.

Who is he? The question went the rounds: Who is Mr Robert Escrick? A retired businessman from London. There was no kind of proof that he came from London, it was purely 'guesswork' again. A few people, the sort who would rush to see the result of an aeroplane disaster, now appeared upon the beach daily, looking up curiously at the refurbished coastguard station. But the worst thing was at the weekend when somebody had the nerve to drive along the approach track and park their car at the end of the cliff, climb out and prepare to picnic exactly where they parked about fifty yards from Robert's house.

Robert strolled out casually, though he was preparing his own lunch, and told them mildly they were on private land. But were they? Does not the cliff-edge belong to everybody? However, having seen Robert close to and having had him speak to them quite civilly, and they replying civilly too, their curiosity was assuaged, they slowly stowed away in the boot the basket they had taken out of their car and drove away with a murmured apology.

But then, while he ate his lunch, he saw two other cars draw up, evidently a party, and before he finished his lunch a great spread was laid out on a tablecloth. Robert poured himself a glass of port; it was important to keep very calm. As he had learned at thirteen, it never pays to lose your temper, never. However, it was very difficult not to do so.

And why was he losing his temper rapidly for the first

time in forty-six years? Because people were coming to trespass upon his land within yards of his home? No doubt people had picnicked on this spot since long before the days of cars started; it was he himself who should take the blame for not assuring that he did not live in a place where this invasion could happen in fine warm weather.

The spell of fine weather lasted for another fortnight and during this period it gradually dawned upon Robert that it was not altogether innocent people who came. Some brought no food and drink but simply sat and stared at his house, watching and waiting for Robert to appear.

Careful observation from the rocking-chair furthest from the window but facing it, taught Robert, up to a point, which were the natives and which the holiday-makers who were not local. And during the weekend of Whitsuntide or thereabouts, a period called Spring Holiday, there was very nearly a crowd on the top of the cliff, and one little cross-eyed girl came with a teapot in her hand and asked for hot water, which Robert kindly gave her, tingling with self-respect.

Half amused and partly rueful, he decided that all this had been sent to 'try' him. You can't have a life which is void of suffering, he told himself; the pain that I am enduring now is good for my character. I must prove that, even at my age, I can and will reconsider and amend.

So as every day passed, he refrained from rushing snarling to a solicitor to seek advice as to how the bloody populace could be prevented from enjoying the access to the sea and the sky that he himself enjoyed.

He mellowed, began to fancy himself as a benevolent old gent, smiling benignly at the squeal of the transistors.

All this benevolence could have gone too far and rendered our hero a simple, daft old ass had there not been, from a distance, a vision of the Blessed Virgin approaching the citadel upon a mule, or rather, upon a small long-haired and dusty donkey. So charming did it look from a distance that Robert took out his binoculars to inspect more closely. As the rider, a woman, was sidesaddle, her strangely angled legs looked pretty and normal in pale blue jeans; there was a big basket on her arm and, alas, the Robert inside Robert refused to admit that he knew exactly who it was.

So he let her ride slowly down the slope at his end of the track from the road. He let her pass within yards of Zoygate and ride, still slowly, through what he now referred to as 'the crowded' cliff edge so that many picnickers and mere observers looked up and watched her pass, some of them shouting recognition or raising their hands in greeting as someone from the same village will.

And having ridden the full length of the occupied territory, she turned and came across the tufty, springy scrub towards his house. Unfortunately she looked directly through his windows as she passed and he had no doubt that she saw him; he could not now pretend to be out.

He sat rigid with terror until he could hear the bang of the door-knocker.

There was no porch to his front door so he knew that she had not dismounted but was leaning forward to catch hold of the knocker. Deliberately he walked quietly to the door and flung it open so that she might be so shocked she fell off. But no! She kept her seat and smiled at him with that chilly, sidelong smirk, and though the sun was shining enough to illuminate ordinary blonde hair, hers now looked grey, grey and lank, and hung down dispirited.

He stepped out and slammed his door behind him, too loudly as it happened. It made such a slam that heads were turned in their direction because the noise of the door drew attention to the scene with a sound above the mild shushing of the waves below, where it was now full tide (which, of course accounted for the increased number of people upon the cliff top).

She held forward the shallow basket which contained a number of shell boxes for him to see. In sheer politeness Robert leaned towards it, though he had no interest in shell boxes whatever, which are essentially a woman's plaything. All had labels with the price marked on to which she pointed, first to this, then to that. They were, in fact, beautifully matched, attractive baubles and finished with dozens of tiny pink shells in two rows, identical, to complete the pattern. He did not for a moment believe that Biddy Hallow had made them. The loving watchful grandmother probably bought them from someone else, Biddy re-selling them.

To get rid of her, he took four boxes, collected in his hands, carelessly in a way shell boxes should never be treated; he backed and kicked at the door backwards with his foot. Of course it didn't open because he had slammed it; he was obliged to put the boxes temporarily back into the basket. She watched with horror as he simply dropped them all together on top of the carefully arranged display. He bolted into the house, found adequate money and returned, handing it to her while she fussily picked out the ones he had not chosen but decided to take. In this effort she slipped to the ground, steadying herself against the passive donkey and shoving the basket under it to be out of the way. When Robert again had his hands full of shell boxes she made her legs into a kind of tripod, stood on tiptoe and flung her arms round his neck. She was so much smaller than he that she took off and simply hung round his neck, trying to reach his mouth, apparently to kiss it.

Robert simply let go of the shell boxes, kicking them, right and left out of the way. She seemed not to have noticed this and went on clinging. Robert lifted his two hands and, putting them on her two skinny shoulders, he prised her off. She staggered back against the donkey, which had not been paying attention and lurched sideways awkwardly; whereupon Biddy Hallow could not but fall on her back over the basket of shells and under the donkey, which, trying to right itself, stood with one small hoof on her face. Giving his door a bigger slam than ever before, Robert vanished behind it, shuddering, swearing and trying to find his handkerchief in order to rub off the hideous and unwelcomed kiss.

He could not find it but hurried to the bathroom where he filled the hand basin with water and washed his face thoroughly, still shuddering. What a damnably incredible, altogether revolting misadventure, and even now he could hear voices outside the door, apparently kind observers were helping.

Robert picked up the bathroom tumbler which he used for cleaning his teeth. Back in the living-room he poured himself out half a tumbler of excellent port; he drank it, not sipping but gulping, and poured out another two inches of port to the sound of the door being rapped constantly.

He walked to the door. Sir Robert Cravenhead was himself again. He flung it open suddenly so that one of those providing instant succour fell backwards inside. He pushed everyone aside and righted her whom he could not refrain from thinking of as 'Twitty Woo', not roughly but firmly. While somehow still holding the bathroom tumbler, he lifted her back on the donkey, where she pretended that she could not sit straight and was supported by several pairs of hands. Her face seemed miraculously the same and there were no traces of serious injury but she was moaning. 'Who is responsible for this girl?' he asked the rescue band.

No answer. Blank looks from one to another.

'Somebody should be looking after her,' he said firmly as he heard a small shell box crunching to pieces beneath his foot. 'Pick up those,' he commanded someone as though to a vassal. 'And now, girl, some of my best port for you.' He took hold of her hair, not cruelly but with authority. She was still snivelling and wailing but she stopped and opened her mouth. Robert poured the port into it. She choked and coughed spectacularly, but she liked the taste. The little crowd stood waiting anxiously for the result, which was almost instantaneous. 'More,' she said, distortedly and loudly, the first word she had uttered which Robert had so far understood.

He went inside and poured out another inch. 'Now,' he

said, handing it to her, 'after this you must go.' He watched her drink it; he took back the glass and looked about at the now scattered helpers. 'Please will someone drive the girl home? She lives in Carrioth.' He looked round: 'And someone else might give themselves the pleasure of riding the donkey back.' He chose a girl of about fifteen, who was looking eager and anxious.

'Ask your parents if you may, right? Now, scatter everybody. Everything's under control.'

'Yes, sir,' a man's voice said respectfully.

Robert went inside and shut the door behind him carefully, not slamming it this time, but locking it, to show he was not going to reappear.

He had decided that he must cut down on the amount of whisky he was pouring into Roundstone, but this Monday, after what Robert thought of as The Scene yesterday, was not the time to do it. He had fully intended to tell Roundstone about the scene with the girl on a donkey, but it seemed that Roundstone already knew everything there was to know and this surprised Robert, since he had assumed that Roundstone led a solitary life.

Far from it, it would appear.

No sooner was the whisky glass in his hand than Roundstone said: 'Now Robert, me boy, what have you been up to? Eh? What sort of new-style rapist have we here?'

'No sort. Rape isn't my dish at all. In fact it would come at the bottom, the very last in a list of crimes I might commit. And furthermore, with an idiot girl . . . tcha! It makes me retch. These Land's Enders seem to live an isolated life, quite out of touch.'

'They used to be part of France, Brittany, man. That accounts for it.'

'That wasn't exactly last year, – ' Robert cried. 'It was only a clean million or so years ago. They should have grown out of that by now!' He started to say something else but Roundstone interrupted him. 'Ssh, I'm thinking.'

After a while he said: 'Now listen: I've been here seven years and more and I'm still a stranger in these parts. I won't be "one of us" till I've been here twenty years. But these seven years I've been observing, watching how they do, if you know what I mean, how their minds work . . . or don't work. Where you went wrong – now don't take offence – it was mere chance, chance it was, that brought you here at the same time that Biddy Hallow, who shouldn't have been anywhere near, gets herself raped, to an exploratory extent. There is no doubt whatever she came here to Zoygate as a sightseer; the whole village has been watching the remarkable transformation from henhouse to minor mansion. And it wasn't quite mindless staring; what was being done here was giving them some ideas of what, in their small way, they might do with their own tumbledown shacks.'

'Um,' which meant go on.

Roundstone drained his glass and banged it down noisily to attract attention to its emptiness.

'Well . . . go on,' Robert encouraged as he refilled it.

'There's many men in this old world never has the smell of a woman from one Christmas to the next.'

'What on earth's Christmas go to do with it?'

'I only mention Christmas because that's a time of the year when sex is at a very low ebb . . .' Robert stared fixedly at him: how serious was he? Then he said he would have thought the exact opposite applied and Roundstone did not reply but looked thoughtful, as though he was about to tell something to Robert but decided against it. 'I should have thought,' Robert said, 'that the month of May would be the rapist's month, the sap rising . . .' He spoke only to encourage Roundstone to continue, not to add irrelevant and vapid thoughts to the discussion. 'However,' he went on, 'that appalling woman was here when I arrived, she was shaking with terror in the bolted lavatory, as you know. No basket. No donkey.'

'Are you referring to our Biddy Hallow?'

'Of course. Who else?'

'I just don't recognize the thing you call her, "appalling woman". That's not Biddy. She's a warm-hearted . . .'

'Over-sexed . . .'

'Yes.' Roundstone readily agreed on that. 'Over-sexed all right, but warm-hearted too and what's wrong with that?'

A thought froze Robert when he remembered that for all Roundstone's pontificating he was getting on for twenty years younger than Robert. It was a case of one man of the world talking to another, and regarding Biddy Hallow, Robert's own claim to be a man of the world was suspect. A great many machine tool makers, contemporaries of Robert's, were pitifully immature when it came to the actual business of living and, indeed, Robert could detect this same immaturity in himself. Happily married he had been for over thirty years, a good father, a man who was scrupulously faithful to his wife. What, in fact, did he know about the world and more particularly about the lives of others?

He had, he was aware, something to learn from Roundstone.

He said: 'How do you come to know Biddy Hallow?'

And Roundstone said: 'We're both beachcombers. I couldn't fail to know her very well indeed. I've taken her sailing on the open sea in a fourteen-foot half-decked cutter; she's as brave as a lion and a good hand with the tiller. Her father, Bart Hallow, was a bit of a bad lot, he died of the drink, but Biddy . . . it's my own opinion "a sea-maid spawned her" (Shakespeare).'

Robert was surprised.

'So you see, Robert, me boy, you've got to take this in the right spirit. You've come to this place out of the blue, nobody knows who you are other than your name. You're quite alone and you're uncommunicative. The first hour you're here, Biddy is found . . . well, there's no need to repeat it all. But there's no history of this kind of thing in the village of Carrioth; it may well have happened but nobody's known about it, or should I say, it's never been a public thing. And happened to our dear Biddy! Television-soaked though we all are, this is still a marvel, a real life marvel, *here*.'

'So?'

'So all you've got to do is to let it flow over you . . .' He waved his hand vaguely. 'Let them have their real life thrill . . . it will blow over. The last one was last year when the bell fell out of the church tower, said to be the result of the Parson messing about with it, though what exactly he was doing, nobody knows. It was a tenor bell and it killed the church cat.'

There was a long pause during which Robert stared down into his glass, swinging it round and sipping, and swinging it again. And looking up, he suddenly caught Roundstone's eye. His look quite clearly asked the question, Who and What are you? Robert had received a distinctly suspect account of who and what Roundstone was, so now he had no intention of telling him anything about himself. In itself, to have a title can cause a stir of interest; Robert had no pride whatever in his knighthood; if it had come to him as a playwright, a poet, an author or an artist, he would have been proud indeed, but as a rich and successful manufacturer it meant nothing whatever to him.

He did, in fact, wonder for a moment how Roundstone would react if he were to say: 'As a matter of fact (which words always presage an uncertainty of mind), *as a matter of fact, I'm a K.*'

'A what?'

'A knight.'

He denied himself the pleasure of being proved right about the way Roundstone would react. He remained po-faced and stared at Roundstone and Roundstone stared back at him and both knew that Robert would tell nothing. But still, since Robert had the subject in mind he could not fail to wonder why there was no mention in *The Times* or, it would seem, any other paper, that he had vanished.

Why was there no outcry? What were his family up to?

Were they sparing his feelings or their own? *Vanished without trace!* Another knight had done this not so long ago and it had become almost a parlour game to guess what had become of him. But the excitement died down and two and a half years later, when he was found dead and dusty from natural causes in an attic in his own house, it did not make any news worth mentioning. If he could remain incognito for two and a half years and was finally discovered to be living happily on a cliff in Cornwall there would be hardly a quiver of interest and his family would be spared much anguish and publicity. Angela would like it that way.

Angela . . .

Soon he would have to write that letter.

He stood up. 'No, I'm not going to give you a drop more whisky,' he told Roundstone, 'but I am going to smoke us both a mackerel each.'

Roundstone much enjoyed his meal and later, when they had washed up and cleared away the smoking oven, Robert looked at his watch: still only half past eight. 'Shall I run you home?'

'Thanks, but there's no need for that.'

'I'd like to.'

'No need at all . . .' He waved the idea away.

But Robert was determined that he was going to see Roundstone's pad. 'Well, Banjo and I will walk back with you,' he said firmly.

'Well, since you're determined to come, thanks, you can come just so far.'

'And no further? Come off it. You've shown me, up to a point, where you live; I could easily find it if I wanted to. What's wrong with it?'

But Roundstone was not taking this light-heartedly. 'It'll make you wonder,' he said slowly and thoughtfully, 'how I happen to have come down in the world.'

'Down in the world?' Robert repeated thoughtfully. 'Have you ever been to Malaysia as a salesman?'

Roundstone shook his head.

'Or the Philippines?'

'No.'

'Or Kuwait?'

'No, I have not.' Roundstone was getting annoyed. 'Have you?'

'Yes, I've been to Kuwait.'

Painfully, Roundstone saw the light.

'You're convincing, when you mean to be,' Robert remarked. 'What about the "daughter busy having babies in Brighton"?'

'Shut up, will you?'

'And the wife a buyer in a London store? No, no, I'm sorry. But I must congratulate you on the casual and therefore persuasive way you threw it all off.'

'What are you going to do, then?'

'Do? Why, nothing but admire and, if we are to remain on good terms, take my soundings, as you might say. Take note that you have associated with people like the person you described yourself to be, a boat-builder with the reliable old family foreman who went and died. Answer me just one question. Roundstone . . . is that your name?'

'Yes.'

'Then we're quits.'

To show he did not wish to talk any more Roundstone picked up his accordion and played to enchant Robert with 'When Irish Eyes Are Smiling' and 'Where the Mountains of Mourne Come Down to the Sea'. He nodded his head slightly in time to the tunes and his shining brown beak made him look, in the failing light, like some predatory bird at feeding time. He got up, finally, saying nothing and left, still saying nothing, and it was not because he was in any sort of temper, Robert understood, but just because there was nothing more he wished to say, and he would rather be alone.

I think he's a scoundrel, went Robert's thoughts, but I'm not sure. And as Roundstone disappeared down the shore path he was playing 'The Wearing of the Green'.

But Irish, Robert thought in mitigation.

CHAPTER VII

My dear Angela,
    You will now have been home about four weeks and will have had time to assess the situation which you will have found there. I don't think it will be a shock or a very great surprise since we have been growing apart these last ten years, have we not? You have made me a wonderful wife and I shall continue to be grateful always.

He read it through, felt encouraged. Went for a walk on the sands, to the east rather than the west, the west being the Biddy Hallow territory. Returned to re-read the letter. Still thought it was the best yet but not good enough; he tore it up and put a match to the fragments as they lay in the hearth.
    Why had he left the letter to Angela so long, until it was to be the last thing he did in the smooth-running plan for his exit? It had become so much more difficult than he had expected:

> I thought when love for you died, I should die.
> It's dead. Alone, most strangely, I live on.

and he thought:

>   . . . Each crawling day
> Will pale a little your scarlet lips, each mile
> Dull the dear pain of your remembered face

and felt both cynical and sick and put his mouldering thoughts down to symptoms of dotage. And then he heard the sound of a somewhat elderly car outside, one more confounded sightseer, no doubt. He flung open the door to greet the visitor with a shocking scowl, but it was the parson from Carrioth and he was stepping from his car with a very sober expression on his face.

'Mr Escrick,' he started off immediately, 'I have come to protest . . .'

'You mean, I seem to have got myself into the lime-light. Well, I do assure you, that it is no wish of mine. My only aim in coming to live here is peace and quiet; to be left alone to pursue certain reading that I have neglected all my life. I am a retired man, all passion spent!' And though Mr Crester deplored any mention of passion, he could not but admire the way this fine-looking man spoke, with what authority, too.

There was a pause as the parson began, unwillingly, to take the side of this unfortunate newcomer. He was surprised at himself and did not have a ready answer. 'I . . . I have to look after my flock,' he stammered at last.

'Of course, but why don't you keep your flock under control? Did you actually preach about casting the first stone after my visit to you? No, I bet you didn't.' Banjo was sniffing suspiciously round Mr Crester's black and shabby trouser-legs.

Robert was thinking of asking him in for a drink when the unhappy man gabbled the most outrageous, in fact the most humiliating, remark that had ever been addressed to Robert.

He actually said with, it must be admitted, the very best of intentions: 'I am asking Mrs Clare to come up and see you: a widow, she has a cottage in the harbour and is a part-time social worker. I think we have problems here with which she alone, of us all in my little community, could deal. It was my wife's idea; she is a cripple, you know, but from her sick bed she is able to help me greatly in these kinds of problem, not that I have many . . .' At the change in Robert's countenance, Mr Crester faltered, he felt he could not be saying the right thing and petered out.

Robert saw red; he could easily have picked up this holy busybody by the back of his clerical collar, walked the fifty yards to the cliff edge and flung him over, not, of course, that he would have very far to fall. The look on his face frightened Mr Crester into immediate action; he backed rapidly into his two-seater Morris Oxford, of which, fortunately, he had left the door open, swung the vehicle round so closely that the wheels gave a shriek of anguish which relieved its owner's feelings considerably, and bumped off up the approach slope as fast as the car would go, which was not fast at all. At the summit of the slope he looked anxiously back to see if he was being followed, but Mr Escrick had disappeared, only Banjo was half-heartedly loping after the visitor.

He's a bit mad, Mr Crester thought. He frightens me. I could believe anything of him. I really don't think it fair to ask Mrs Clare to come up here. He might murder, upon my soul, he might!

In his cottage Robert felt he had achieved a job of self-exorcism and regained his shredded sense of humour. He laughed, not very loud or very long, but he laughed. And now, stepping across to the window, he saw Roundstone's red sail a mile or so out, and, taking Banjo, he set off to find Roundstone's pad and he put a torch in his pocket in case he was still searching as darkness fell. He knew that Roundstone would quite often, when the sea was reasonably calm, not return till dawn and Roundstone himself had explained this by telling of the fun of fishing by artificial light, and had expatiated upon the excitement of the tiny monsters from the deep who would swim into view and often into his net.

'You must take me along with you one day,' Robert had suggested enthusiastically.

'Yes, yes indeed!' Roundstone had concurred liberally, 'I'll do that, I certainly will.' But any more insincere agreement Robert never wished to hear.

So now he tramped off down the path to the shore; the tide was ebbing almost to turning-point, but not quite. It was safe to go the shore way until he was, by his own reckoning, exactly below the new coastguard's station, then climb one of the cliff paths. It would be easier, the first time, than tramping overland across the moorland gorse and bracken which, somehow, could be daunting when the actual object to be attained was out of sight.

From where Roundstone had first shown him the new coastguard's station he saw it once more, and knowing that he could not fail to find it, he confidently set out. As he walked he looked carefully, not out to sea, but at the ragged cliffs to his left, the giant rocks flung haphazard all along the beach, many hid the view of cave entrances; there were juttings out of the cliff and bites of the coast making small private bays which once used to entrance the odd visitor who could bathe naked on the deserted shore with impunity; now at the height of the season the official Life-Saver patrolled the coast in a rowing-boat to save visitors from their own idiocy as well as shoot down indecency in the form of naked bathing. (Well, not exactly *shoot*.)

Finally he knew he had almost arrived because he saw the tip of the mast of the coastguard's station, holding no storm cones this mild summer's evening, and the little jetty. He found, too, the rugged zigzag path up the cliff.

This station was a Day Watch one which was manned only during daylight by four watchmen, each taking four-hour stretches; three of their cars were parked on the gravel approach and it would seem that unless there was exceptionally bad weather, there would be no one on duty in the hours of darkness.

A couple of hundred yards away he could see what must be Roundstone's hut. He could see someone moving about in the look-out, but no attention was paid to Robert as he skirted the actual Government property and made his way to the hut across the scrub.

It was locked, as he might have expected, but there was a sizeable window the top sections of which dropped open some foot or so to let in air. Robert rolled up a large stone and stood on it, holding his hands to the sides of his eyes so that reflection did not prevent him seeing at least something.

It was like the cabin of a First Officer, but there were no

photographs, nor, from the narrow view he had across
the bed which was built in like a bunk under a porthole,
was there anything personal whatever, other than the
accordion which hung on its strap from a big clothes hook
behind the door. There was a radio on view but no
cooking appliances, a store cupboard was visible from
where he stood, and the place was impressively clean and
in excellent condition. Not a small crease marred the
surface of the spotless white counterpane.

Later Robert was to wish that he had been able to see
what hung against the wall behind the top of the bunk,
which was built against the window through which he was
looking. The crucifix might have thrown some clue to
Roundstone. There was nothing to identify, and he failed
to understand why Roundstone had not wanted him to
see it unless he was ashamed of its exceeding modesty
compared with Robert's habitat. He walked away
disappointed that he was no wiser from the visit, which
told him no more about Roundstone than he already knew.

But as he retraced his steps towards the path back the
way he had come, since the tide would not yet have
advanced far up the sands, he noticed a man come out of
the station and raise the bonnet of his car, preparatory,
presumably, to filling his battery with distilled water.
Robert went across and spoke to him: Was this the place
where a man of the name of Roundstone was employed?

Yes, indeed it was.

Would it be possible to speak to him?

Not if he's not over there, in his hut.

Um, pity. 'I'm wondering if he has any spare time, to
do a bit of digging for me?'

'He works for us.'

'Full time?'

He was not prepared to answer that in case he was
indiscreet. The man slammed down the bonnet of his car
irritably and asked who was Robert, anyway. Robert told
him he had been living in Zoygate, over there, for some
weeks or so. He had bought it and intended to live
there.

The man looked at him with interest.

'Yes,' he said in a friendly manner, 'well, you might well get Roundstone to do a bit of work for you, he's hale and hearty. Shall I tell him you called?'

'No thanks, I saw him recently; this is a sudden idea I had. I'm certain to meet him on the beach again fairly soon.'

Robert sauntered off thoughtfully.

Sometimes Roundstone was out all night; there had been a wondrous full moon last week, for instance, and Robert, taking out his binoculars to identify a speck on the horizon, recognized it as Roundstone's boat which he had described as of doubtful class but sound performance. And later, when Robert got up to start his day, he looked out of the window to find, not the kind of fog he had experienced the first few days he came, but a fairly thick morning mist presaging a hot day; an ideal condition in which to land, for instance, illegal immigrants who, Robert had read recently in the paper, had increased in numbers by over a thousand last year, in spite of continual watch along the whole coast.

It was not that Robert had any wish to harm his newly found friend, it was simply that retirement had not just brought down a lid over Robert's alertness of mind. He was under no obligation now, to think about any machine tool whatever, but he was at liberty to think, in a wondering, constructive way about the activities of anyone he might meet.

But if he were to find that Roundstone smuggled itinerant Asians into the country, what was he, Robert, going to do about it?

He had no plans, he just wanted to find out if it were so.

Two evenings later Roundstone was along for his whisky. He also brought Robert a present which Robert liked very much indeed: a large piece of smoked salmon. Roundstone explained that it was all he felt he could bring to someone without a deep-freeze; he himself took advantage of the freezer at the station which was stocked with food used in bad weather when there had to be constant watch.

'So you saw my pad?'

'I looked through the window.'

'Oh!'

'Were you ashamed of its modesty?'

'Maybe.'

'Don't be. It's fine. But too small to have visitors.'

'And I'm told you were after me for some work?'

'Yes,' Robert agreed, 'I was. I think something will have to be done with my frontage, as the lawyers call it. I have found out from the plan exactly how far my land stretches towards the cliff edge and I think something should be done to make it look as though it belongs to somebody up to a certain point; not a garden, of course, that could not be attempted in this sort of situation, but removal of the brushwood and the stunted growth. That silvery sort of grass which grows on sandhills might possibly thrive.'

'And a fence round?'

'Certainly not. No fence would stand up to the wind, I'm sure . . .'

Roundstone chuckled: 'But it might deter the sight-seers. But don't get yourself too worried about the so-called sightseers. Since I have been here there has been an immeasurable increase in holiday-makers; at one time there was talk of a caravan park and speculators were mouching round, but this is far too exposed a spot.'

'So you are prepared to tackle this bit of land, are you?'

'If you'll pay me current wages?'

'Of course.'

'I did a job of that kind over at the Station. If you've got a rough lawn in mind, stop thinking about it; that couch grass is hell with long spreading roots and damn well cuts your hands when you try to pull it up. But I can get all the rest of the stuff moved and see how it goes.' Roundstone took the small round stone out of his pocket and fiddled with it.

'Tell me,' Robert said, 'what are you really, don't tell me you're a gardener by profession!'

'Why should I? You don't tell me a word about what your profession is; you keep me guessing; I bet it's some kind of . . .' He paused. 'Certainly not a businessman. A Civil Servant, perhaps. You might even be an army man. A general?'

Robert laughed with gusto; this was becoming ridiculous. If there was to be no public interest whatever in the missing knight, what on earth did it matter what he did for a living? 'I'm a machine tool maker, if you must know; so you're wrong on all points and a rotten bad guesser. Do you even know what exactly a machine tool manufacturer manufactures? No, you don't, of course, so I won't bother to tell you. It's something I've never really had at heart. I like people better than tools. I should have done something that involved people.'

'Like . . . being a parson?'

'No, not like being a parson . . . like being a curator, perhaps. Or a professor.'

'What a curious idea. A curator is more keen on things than people.'

'I see myself arranging things in a museum, that's true, but then I'd have the interest of seeing how people react to what I've done!'

'So yes, I do notice you're interested in people, like going over to see my pad, out of sheer curiosity.' As he spoke he was not holding his glass but in his fingers was the tiny stone which he was turning over and over; his legs were crossed and he was swinging one carelessly. He said: 'If you really want to know, I'm an eavesdropper.'

'A gossip, in other words. That's why you knew all about me and that Biddy Hallow . . .'

Two more whiskies on they were talking politics, capping one another's opinion regarding Government behaviour. 'So it's the age of mistakes, every decision made seems to be the wrong one . . .'

'I'm not for any Government,' Roundstone boasted.

'You must be, since you've had some reasonably sound things to say.'

'I'm an anarchist.'

'I see, so you're for Revolution.'

'Yes!'

'God help me! You're not having another whisky!'

'What do *you* think an anarchist is?'

'An absolute b – '

'An anarchist is one who undermines repression.'

'That sounds very fine.'

'Freedom!', Roundstone said.

'Do you not consider yourself free?'

'I'm free. It's others who are not.'

Robert fixed him with a hard cold stare. 'You're surely ... you cannot be talking about Ireland?'

'Of course I am. What else?'

'Born in a font! Of course ... you must be an Irishman. I begin to see the light.'

'How do you mean?' Roundstone snarled.

'It must have been an Irishman who put you there. Anyone else would have left you on the steps round the font, but your probable parent took the trouble to lift the heavy lid off the font and put you inside ... to make sure his son was brought to God's notice!'

'If it wasn't so serious,' Roundstone said, 'I'd laugh!'

'And I'll tell you what,' Robert went on, 'it's not freedom for your countrymen you're bothered about, it's freedom from your own, your very own, inherited and inborn misapprehensions regarding the word freedom.'

'By God! Give me back my piece of smoked salmon!'

'Certainly not. I shall eat it, enjoying the freedom you have given me to do so!'

When Roundstone had staggered off into the whispering night, Robert made a smoked salmon sandwich and took it to bed, where he opened the diary of Parson Kilvert whom he much admired as a diarist of the last century, who lived in wildest Welsh border country. In planning his future Robert had decided upon writing a diary of day-today *Observations from a Cliff-Top* as he intended to call it. But he was discouraged to find his own life on the cliff falling sadly short of Kilvert's. He read that:

Nov. 16 Last night the waning moon shone bright and cold in the East and I had a horrible dream that I was married to Mrs Danzey and living as curate at Gwythian; I woke up in a cold sweat. This morning I learned of the death of Mrs Augustus Hare . . .

Nov. 17 Went to see young Meredith who had his jaw locked for six months, a legacy of mumps. He has been to Hereford Infirmary where they kept him two months, gave him chloroform and wrenched his jaws open gradually by a screw lever. But they could not do him any good.

But next evening, supported by another smoked salmon sandwich, he sat down and wrote a day of his diary, to try it out.

June 18 Battle of Waterloo. Late this afternoon I found myself run out of butter so had to go into Carrioth to get some. I picked my way carefully with Biddy Hallow very much in mind, watching to right and to left, making sure that every object in sight was not Biddy. There were two fishermen sitting with their backs against an upturned boat. There was a father playing cricket with his small sons; there were two old ladies knitting on the shingle and there was an artist, well, that no doubt is how she would refer to herself, sitting at an easel opposite a group of boats and nets on the hard dry sand.

I bought my butter and came away. I was not stoned, nor pointed at, nor, in fact, remarked in any way though I was wearing my dirty cream jeans and espadrilles, my thick-knit navy pullover and my dark glasses. So back on the beach I went up to the girl painting and looked at her canvas from behind her by about five feet. She knew I was there. And when I stopped staring in horror at what she was drawing and painting, I appraised her figure which was really something.

I admired the bathing suit which was either very old in fashion or very new. Whichever it was, it showed her superb figure to perfection, unlike those postage-stamp-sized bits of material which the modern girl hangs about herself in three relevant places and which bemuse the eye of the beholder so much that he cannot correctly assess the value of the girl's body as a whole. This girl might have been wearing her grandmother's bathing suit, it ended below the knee and had sleeves to her wrist and it was unrelieved black so that I felt like asking her if she were in mourning. She knew damn well I was standing behind her and I moved more closely because I could not believe what she was making of the boats and the net. She turned round slowly and I was a pushover, or I should say, I lost my balance with the shock of seeing the most large, shining, wide-open, heavily lashed eyes I have ever seen. She smiled and turned back to her work, saying nothing while I wobbled to a standstill and stood staring. I was not going to be the first to speak and it seemed . . . nor was she. Presently I called Banjo who was having the whale of a time with the small boys, and we walked away.

So last night I dreamed . . . but no, I must not tell my dreams, like Parson Kilvert.

June 19   Saw her again, stood a quarter of an hour, she looked at me once and said nothing. Nor did I. I must write to Angela. I must, I must.

June 20   Ditto.

June 21   Ditto.
Midsummer Day, a cold wind blowing. Banjo was sick after eating a dead crab.

June 22   Ditto, only I have discovered that she had not been using the same paper, or whatever she uses; she has changed it several times, but is still at the same scene except that the two fishermen are posing for her!

Tomorrow, come what may, I shall somehow or other examine Roundstone's boat.

So Robert realized that he had, as he thought, made a fool of himself; five times running he had walked to the same spot at the same time to look at the female artist who sat exactly in the same place each day. On the sixth day he took his binoculars and stood on the cliff a mile from the spot where she had sat near the upturned boat, and this time there was no girl, no easel or stool and no fishermen.

His diary was not that of a happily occupied man and he flinched at the thought that he might not be making a success of the way of life that had been planned for so long.

On the third day after he had seen the painter on the beach, Roundstone came in the mid-morning with a sickle, saying that he had come to start work on the ground in front of Robert's cottage. Stricken with a vague shame that he would not dare to swing a sickle in the way in which Roundstone was doing, Robert whistled Banjo up and they set off down the cliff path and took the direction to the east where Robert guessed one of the caves hid Roundstone's boat. Today the tide was going out rapidly, it crashed vigorously on to the rocks and ebbed with chuckling trickles, which was pleasant enough but made the rocks slippery and it was slow going. With every twist and turn of the rocky coastline there was an unfamiliar scene, each differed from the other, and to have explored each and every cave would take weeks. However, he rounded one particularly sharp outstanding rock to see Roundstone's boat rocking gently at a shallow anchorage a little way out; it was surprising that he should have left the red, wet sails in an untidy heap on the sand. There was still too much water for him to be able to paddle out to it, so he lay down in a crevice of rock while Banjo pottered about, occasionally putting one paw in a pool in a playful attempt to catch something.

It was pleasantly warm and sheltered and an hour passed while Robert slept for a time. He awakened to the sound of voices; two men were standing a few yards away with their backs to Robert, whom they could barely have seen if they had turned to look. The tide had gone a long way and he could hear what they said.

'. . . every time I see this damn boat, it's the same . . . I think there's no more innocent craft to be found the length and breadth of the peninsula. It's my opinion you've got a bee in your bonnet.'

'The lighthouse has sixty or so miles of heaving water to sweep. As someone said there can be a lot of small sailing boats in sixty miles, man. And as for the coast, you know only too well how long it can be before a corpse turns up.'

'We're not talking about corpses now, it's miscreant boats and how long do you have to know about it before deciding . . .'

They strolled away and Robert could no longer hear what they said. They approached the boat which was lolling sideways as the tide had receded, leaving it high and dry. They stood again, discussing it, nodding heads and raising a hand as one or other made a point. Then, still in consultation, they climbed up the cliff path as though to the station.

Though Robert had not reached the jetty immediately below the coastguard station he thought that they had probably come from there, there were several paths up to it.

So it might seem Roundstone was doing some type of smuggling and was suspected by his employers after how long? Was it seven years? He could not rid himself of the ever-recurring opinion that Roundstone was smuggling drugs. Having no information at all as to how drugs were smuggled into the country in small boats, he was convinced that they did not come in bulk but in quantities manageable by one individual.

He called to Banjo who was now a long way down the beach, swimming in a rock pool, the top of his head and nose only appearing. He came at the double and shook himself liberally over his master.

When they had climbed the cliff path back to Zoygate, they found Roundstone still at it. He had achieved a sizeable pile of brushwood, and was apparently an excellent worker.

'You can knock off for today, and thanks.' Robert was in fact really grateful; there was already a noticeable improvement.

'A lady called to see you,' Roundstone said. 'She's a Mrs Clare, said the Parson had asked her to call. Came in a Mini. I know her, she's a good sort.'

'Tcha! Would you believe it, she's a social worker, sent to sort me out!'

Roundstone's laugh was infectious. 'I had one of them when I first came,' he boasted. 'Up there . . .' He indicated the new coastguard's station with a jerk of his head. 'They thought I was up to no good, an ex-criminal or summat. They sent this female . . . not at all like Mrs Clare . . . oh, she was kind! But she was a long way off the mark, and the more she called, the further off she seemed to go. She packed it in, in the end. But they don't trust me up there, all the same.'

'No, they don't, do they?'

Roundstone swung round on him, serious now. He snarled: 'How do *you* know?'

'Eavesdropping. You said the other day you were an eavesdropper, well . . . so am I! They think you're a smuggler, Roundstone. Are you?'

Roundstone insisted that he repeat the conversation he had overheard. When Robert did so, Roundstone said firmly: 'No, I am not a smuggler and I am sad and sorry you should suspect me. What would I need the money for?'

'If you're not engaged in any kind of smuggling, then I apologize, I feel a fool, indeed I do. I'm not making excuses for my own folly but it's living alone; I'm not used to it. And it's this place!'

'Don't you like it here, then?'

'It's not that I don't like it; I can't somehow . . .' He paused.

'Get your bearings?' Roundstone suggested.

'Not quite that . . . it's . . . I'm not in harmony with the place. It's so new to me and, in a way, strange. I might quite well go a bit mad, old chap. Do me a favour: keep me on the straight.'

'What shall I do the next time this Mrs Clare, the social worker, arrives?'

'Tell her to go to hell.'

'I would never do such an unholy thing to that lady. I think I should tell you these social workers don't come for the fun of it.'

'No?'

'You're not suspected of criminal tendencies so much. They're waiting . . . waiting . . . to help you if you're in trouble . . . kind.'

Robert shuddered. 'We're not living in the Middle Ages. Who are waiting and what for?'

'Middle Ages! This is modern! As far as everybody who lives round here knows, you've committed criminal assault; it's just that they haven't quite been able to pin it down to you so far, the police, I mean; but they're keeping a watch on you all right and in the village of Carrioth they're just about locking up their daughters, believe you me!'

'I can't . . . but go on . . .'

'A visit from the social worker might mean you could confess!'

'For God's sake! Don't be silly!'

'You might have something on your mind you wished to tell her . . .'

Robert ran his hands distractedly through his thick white hair.

Roundstone went on: 'It's modern and civilized, you ought to understand that. I darn nearly shouted after her as she walked away: "Excuse me, but your compassion is showing!" ' '

'Shut up!' Robert shouted.

Later, when Roundstone had gone, he got out his writing-pad. But he was now feeling a very long way from writing to Angela.

Dear Angela . . . he started.

But he had lost touch, not necessarily with Angela but with himself. He, Robert Cravenhead, was no longer himself but another, called Robert Escrick, with whom he was unfamiliar. This Robert Escrick was unpredictable; perhaps he looked a criminal type, the sort who would assault girls in public conveniences. It was quite unrealistic that this new, new weirdy should write a letter to somebody whom he remembered as Angela. He got up and put on a record of Beethoven sonatas instead.

CHAPTER VIII

AND NOW there was one way on the beach he should not take; it was west and Carrioth village stood upon that western shore. He must not meet Biddy Hallow. But, on the other hand, there was that painter-woman, and now seeing her had become more important than not seeing Biddy Hallow. Last time he had seen her she was wearing a bulky cream linen smock, long brown legs stretched out under the easel, as she seemed to be both drawing and painting at the same time, the fishermen lolling at their ease against the upturned boat, one of them smoking one of the short pipes he had noticed before and the other with his shabby coarse straw hat pulled almost over his face.

First he saw Biddy Hallow, and because the tide was right out he could give her a wide berth; she had her big basket with her and she was going from rock pool to rock pool, seeing what new sort of shell the tide had left. Did the shells change from tide to tide? She was so engrossed that she did not see Robert, or possibly did not recognize him because, though barefoot, he was wearing a straw sun hat he had bought in Portugal. Banjo might well have attracted her attention but was far off on the seaward side on some errand of his own. Robert reassured himself that Biddy would do nothing direful so close to the village. He was entirely mistaken in this self-deception, but he was so determined to get to know the woman artist that he threw caution aside.

This morning he astonished himself by going up to her as though they were old friends. He had assured himself that she was a visitor because only these last few mornings had she been there, in the same spot, with her easel, and never before then had he seen her. This morning she had a large flat tin open on her knee and was sharpening what seemed to be her chalks or crayons.

The upturned boats, the fishermen, the artist all arranged like a picture postcard, yet nothing seemed to have been more casual or unarranged.

After the first few remarks about the pleasant morning and the fallen wind, they advanced to talk about painting, water-colours, pastels, charcoal. The fishermen put in a word here and there, they mentioned the number of artists who came over from St Ives for a day's painting a new scene, and one of the fishermen told how another fisherman had been so intrigued that he had started painting himself, made a great sloppy mess of a picture with a big messy sun setting behind a sailing boat, sent it to an exhibition in Penzance and won the third prize for a work by a real Cornishman.

In the course of this Robert said he had come to live at Zoygate and how he too felt he would like to know something about the art of doing – he waved his hand vaguely – this sort of thing; there were such wonderful colours to be seen, sometimes everything pale and misty and sometimes blazing like a scene in the South of France. Etcetera . . . etcetera.

Then Robert strolled on up the village and bought his newspaper which he always managed to pick up from

one or other of the villages he visited regularly. He went
into the local pub for a pint of stout and when he returned
she was settled to work seriously.

'Come up and see my pad,' Robert said very casually.
'It might amuse you to see what I've made of that pile of
stones.'

'Shall I?' The woman did not look up but went on with
her work. 'Maybe I will, since you've asked me.' The
fishermen concealed whatever thoughts they may have
had but were taking in every syllable. It was quite clear
that Robert should go no further with this acquaintance-
ship in front of these keen observers; as soon as he moved
away he felt they would look knowingly at one another
and nod, even more satisfied that they had all agreed
upon something. Before he moved out of range the woman
looked over her shoulder and shouted: 'My name's
Nesta!'

'Thanks, I'll remember,' Robert returned and whistled
to Banjo.

And now Banjo really disgraced himself. Robert was
walking easily with his paper tucked under his arm; he
felt better after his normal conversation with pleasant
people and the stout he had drunk. Relaxed, for the
moment he forgot Biddy Hallow, and so did Banjo, if he
had ever remembered her.

Then Banjo saw what he had seen before and not
understood, this bundle lying beside a pool about two
hundred yards seawards, and went to investigate. She
must have smelled strongly of mermaid because he
pulled enthusiastically at her tattered (deliberately, no
doubt) skirt.

There was no doubt that Biddy Hallow sought shells in
the most unnecessarily abandoned way. Whether or not
she really did have to get herself into that unusual
position when seeking a suitable shell hidden beneath a
curtain of seaweed hanging from a rock, is questionable.
Banjo had to see what it was all about and pressed his
face against hers with the enthusiasm of a dedicated
collector.

It would seem impossible that Robert should have got himself in this sort of situation once again and of course he would not have done so if it had not been for the over-enthusiastic Banjo. Shouting loudly for his dog and whistling, he raced across the space between them, stood still, and Banjo at last heard him and desisted from his exploration, returning meekly to his master and leaving Biddy Hallow in a state of hysteria.

Several people, about seven, visitors and fishermen, rushed to help and once again Robert was aware of terrible humiliation. It was really too squalid; Robert found himself apologizing for his dog who had done nothing other than explore. It fell to the fishermen with whom he had had a friendly talk about paints to pick up Biddy, because Robert could not bring himself to touch her. They carried her back up the slope from shore to village, where a group of people had gathered, of course. The people left standing round the pool waited for some sort of comment from Robert but he hurried away with Banjo depressed at his heels, without a look back, agonizingly asking himself what was wrong with him. Things like this never used to happen. What was it? What pestilence had fallen upon him, he asked himself, what hoodoo had now become his own special evil spirit? The fisherman who had been lounging near the painter had heard him casually picking up the girl. This was some-thing Robert never did; why, when in the circumstances that he found himself with Biddy, did he actually invite the unknown female to Zoygate?

Or was it just bad luck? It must surely have been clear to everybody that the episode had nothing to do with him other than that it was his dog. And it must also be clear that nothing had happened to Biddy Hallow other than that she was easily scared. A country girl ought not to be scared into hysterics by a big playful black labrador. It could not possibly be that Biddy Hallow only had hysterics when Robert was on the scene; there must have been many, many times when the shrill unearthly screams of Biddy assailed the ears of the inhabitants of the village of Carrioth.

The woman Nesta, he remembered noticing, had remained on her stool, her attention focused upon her easel; perhaps she had looked round to see what had happened but at the moment Robert had looked across the two hundred yards of sand, she had been engrossed in her painting or drawing and taken no notice whatever.

So Robert arrived at Zoygate which he had not yet learned to call 'home' and fixed himself a good strong drink and turned on his record-player. And Banjo, satisfied that his master was no longer angry with him, sank down with his paws under his chin, an attitude he struck when he was aggrieved, not raising his head but looking at his master with a stricken look, his eyes fallen back and showing an abnormal amount of white. And Robert remained unaware that it had been sheer unconscious loneliness and the fact that he had not happened to speak to a woman since his arrival.

It seemed strange to receive no letters even though it had been planned thus; these, if any, were delivered into a wooden box fixed at the gap in the main road which was the start of the track to his house, and there was a small rickety piece of wood with ZOYGATE written upon it in very shaky white painted capitals. It was a measure of Robert's total inertia and lack of interest about any mail for him that he had not looked inside the box since he came. He did so now and there were three circulars addressed to The Occupier and that was all. He had kept up his apparent indifference to his family admirably and he could not but feel a certain grudging admiration that they had so totally carried out his expressed wishes. But now, after the first and somewhat mitigated rapture was over, he felt slightly aggrieved that the total vanishing of Sir Robert Cravenhead, whose name so often made headlines in the financial papers, had not made the smallest stir. It was common knowledge that he had retired, but did that really mean sunk without trace?

He looked up at the wild scream of laughter just above him, it was as though the gulls were laughing scornfully. He was still sensitive to their constant jeers, though it was one of the things he had been looking forward to; but now it seemed this particular gull had a message and it was that the young artist from the beach had, as she had promised, come to see him. She came up the beach pathway and stood upon the land which Roundstone had been working on a few days before. She looked round and Robert walked towards her with a pleased smile. 'You've come!' he cried, delighted.

'But what do you think I'm really up to?'

'Coming to see me, I hope.'

'No, that's part of it but what I really want to find is all the places along the cliff where the boys find the gulls' nests. Gulls' eggs have been in season in May and they're much more expensive than they used to be in the shops. I thought I might find some nests for myself with the baby birds in; I might even cruelly loot some eggs next season.'

'Good heavens,' Robert shouted, 'is the year really over the gulls'-egg period? I should have been at my club devouring them. My favourite food!'

It was her favourite food too, and she had pressed the village boys to tell her where the nests were but they did not want to do so because they sold the eggs to dealers, and besides, they said, a lady could not climb about the cliffs where they were found.

'The cottage I'm living in down on the harbour belonged to my husband's family and now it's mine because my husband died so I am a resident here, but not all the time, and even residents don't get let into the gulls' nest circle. It's all part of the crab and lobster corporation, and even that isn't available for ordinary people; the eggs go to Maxim's in Paris and such places.'

'There can't be a shortage of gulls' eggs,' Robert mused, 'because there certainly isn't a shortage of gulls!'

'Availability is the operative word. When you hear things aren't available it simply means: *you're* not going to have any, and that's that!' and they both laughed.

'I haven't been around much since you came. I often go to London, and my Papa took me out to lunch a few weeks ago and we had gulls' eggs and Papa said he would eat them because they were there, but never would he take one from a nest!'

Robert showed her round; she was neither gushing nor enthusiastic but he felt, somehow, that she liked it. Robert told her there was a short list of things which needed to be done but on the whole he was pleased with the builders Brown & Bright and their architect Jack Wither, whom he called a most obliging man. He told her about the time it had taken from first to last and how he had been down here several times during the building, which took about a year.

And after he had showed her everything and poured out a drink for them both, while she stood by the bookshelves and pulled out one here and there, she sat down in one of the rocking-chairs and said nothing. Robert was to learn that she was a woman who could keep quiet for a long time, but he had never met one of those and felt both amazed and uncomfortable that she had no small talk. Though he gave her a few leads, she did not pick them up but sat looking out over the quiet sea with thoughtful great eyes.

'How about trying for some gulls' nests?' she said at last. 'Let's explore. Have you a rope?'

Totally amazed, Robert went to get the rope which he had, in fact, bought but could not now imagine why; he had left it in the car, plastic wrapped, just as he bought it from the camping shop in Albermarle Street.

Then he very much wanted to ask her more things about herself, but felt that if he did so he would have to tell her things about himself in return which he did not wish to do.

When he had torn the packing off the rope he shook it out; there seemed miles of it. 'Come on,' she said, 'don't let's waste time.'

'But surely we're not going to need all this?'

'Hack a piece off, then.'

G

'How long?'

'Hack it in half.'

He was relieved that his knife was in good condition, he would have been ashamed at any blatant inefficiency on his part, frightened of criticism from those beautiful but critical eyes.

In dead silence they walked along the cliff edge, she leading; there was no small talk, indeed, no talk of any kind. The seagulls did the talking in shrill and nagging tones. They walked eastwards towards the new coast-guard's station; it was clear that she knew exactly where she was going and she stopped at a place which was an indentation in the now high cliff, with gulls circling above, screaming warning of enemy approach.

'Now,' she said practically: 'you wind this twice round your middle and give me, say, ten yards to hang on to. This is only a precaution, I've only to go a few feet down . . .'

He looked at her feet: she was wearing pale blue jeans and a loose shirt and on her feet were French espadrilles. She noticed his glance and said these shabby things were the safest for any rock climbing, they were old friends and would not let her down. 'Now, you stand back; I'm not going to disappear from view completely but you won't be able to see me because you're standing a few feet back . . . about here.' And she put her foot where she wished him to stand. 'Don't worry, unless I'm very unlucky there won't be any pull on this rope at all.'

He watched as she vanished from sight over the edge of the cliff and gave a sudden shout of: 'Wow! How mean can we get? There's four teenagers in this nest!' Robert was considerably alarmed that a parent seagull was about to attack her with its beak in addition to the vile language it was casting upon her; rabid curses, no less, joined by others from the encircling crowd. If they were not frightening Nesta, they frightened Robert; he shouted for her while keeping a firm hold on the rope.

She was out of sight about fifty seconds and reappeared smiling triumphantly; she threw down the end of the rope for him to roll up, saying: 'That's it, there're four nests . . . oh dear God! what swine we are!'

On the way back Robert was as silent as he had been on the way there; but now he was suffering from surprise. He had always believed that where women were concerned in any kind of expedition, there was always a lot of noise and fuss. He was experiencing a familiar kind of happiness, the kind that he used to feel when he had solved a tiresome problem satisfactorily; the fact that he had only stood with the rope tightly round him was neither here nor there; the finding of four gulls' nests did not really account for this happiness either.

Back at Zoygate he hoped for a heart to heart talk but there was nothing like that: 'I must fly before it starts to go dark. Thanks for helping me!'

And she was off.

The pip of the horn of a police car a quarter of an hour later was annoying but he felt so happy that he went on chopping onions for a minute. But the brass dolphin on the door insisted that he answer and once again he let in the policemen.

Talk, talk and all so deadly repetitive. So boring, so tiring, so slightly nauseating: how come there was this last . . . er . . . scene upon the almost deserted beach? . . . certainly not deserted, Officer, there were quite a few . . . what would you call quite a few, Mr Escrick? . . . how long have you been here at Zoygate? . . . you know perfectly well, Officer, you were here the second day . . . after you took up residence? . . . and you came from? . . . Officer, I am under no obligation whatever to tell you where I came from and nor are you entitled to ask the question . . . but why not answer? . . . because I do not wish to do so . . . why not? . . . because I have done nothing whatever which justifies your questions, in fact, I am being positively . . . have you ever heard of witch-hunting? . . . well, this persecution of myself amounts to something like that . . . you employ the man Roundstone from the coastguard station? . . . what has that got to do with anything? . . . on and on and on with nobody scoring a point.

There was a younger man who evidently liked Robert, and when the interview became static with getting abolutely nowhere, the senior of the two men appeared to stalk out in a state of irritation. The younger man hung behind.

He said: 'It's not only this Biddy Hallow thing . . .' and he bent to adjust his shoelace so that his lagging behind would not rouse suspicion. 'It's something which has been going on for years actually, not here only but . . .'

The young man seemed to have some difficulty in choosing what he would say but he was clearly motivated by kindness.

'What do you mean . . . ?' Robert started.

'We . . . we've got to . . .'

'Got to *what*?'

There was not one more second to spare, the young officer stood up and moved towards the door. 'Well, good day, sir!' And then, just as he was shutting the door to join his senior who was now sitting waiting in the car, he said one word, and it was unmistakably: '*Anarchy!*'

Robert went back to his onions and mused over them. He felt an enormous relief, the relief of one totally innocent. It was Roundstone they were really after. Roundstone with his admiration for Biddy Hallow and his mysterious activities in his 'fourteen-foot half-decked cutter of doubtful class but sound performance'. Roundstone who had been here seven years. Roundstone the holy terror. A subversive Roundstone. A man who smoothly described anarchy as 'something which undermines repression'.

What was he going to do?

Help the ineffectual policemen for whom, out of sheer irritation, Robert wrongly had conceived contempt?

Or help Roundstone who, it seemed, was a pretty ineffectual anarchist and an admirer of a half-witted nymphomaniac?

CHAPTER IX

THREE DAYS PASSED during which his initial pleasure and relief turned to worry about being what was called *under interrogation*; no law-abiding man really feels comfortable under this threat. *Helping the police with their enquiries* means the same thing but has not the slightly threatening sound that the first has. *Under interrogation:* it repeated itself over and over again in his mind and quite prevented him from enjoying the rest of the smoked salmon which Roundstone had given him.

Then, on the afternoon of the third day he saw his artist friend Nesta standing on the edge of the cliff with her back to the sea, looking at his house. She had her sketch-book under her arm and a charcoal pencil in her hand and she tapped her front teeth thoughtfully as she looked. And then she walked somewhat nearer and started to sketch the building, Robert went out, he could not disguise his pleasure.

'Hallo, Robert Escrick,' she said without looking up, 'I'm doing this, it will be finished in a minute.'

And when she held it up for him to see he could not at first see how it differed from the actual appearance of the house at the moment except that it looked extremely pleasant.

'Don't you *see*?'

He shook his head. 'I'm terribly dense, have you changed it somehow?'

'The door!' she cried. 'The combined front and back door. It's too narrow, it gives the house a prim look!'

'Good heavens! We can't have that!' He snatched the sketching-pad from her and studied it. 'But you're right! How did I come to miss that?'

'It's not that I don't like the whole building, I like it, but a double door twice the present width would give it that touch of . . . luxury, don't you think?'

Once Robert had decided that the door must be altered, even though everything had been approved and paid for, he wanted to get on with the alteration immediately and he asked Nesta to come with him in the Range Rover to the architect's office which was beside the building yard ten or so miles away.

She agreed to this and, Banjo left on guard, they drove off.

Though work was going on in the building yard Jack Wither was not there; the girl in the office said Mr Wither was expected back in half an hour as he had an appointment at three.

'We'll wait,' Robert said.

They strolled about for twenty minutes or so and when they returned to the yard a noise of saws attracted them to the carpenter's shed where much was going on, and among the workers he saw a familiar face. It was Fred Bedfont whose upper half was a striking sight: he was naked to the waist and a mahogany brown; he wore a tiny tangerine coloured vest from the armholes of which his spectacular shoulders appeared; but his vest had shrunk in the wash so that his large hairy navel was visible just above the top button of his jeans.

He greeted Robert in a way vaguely reminiscent of an old school chum. 'Everything all right, then? Not come to complain, I hope, have you?'

Short of snubbing, Robert felt compelled to tell him why he had come.

'Hell's bells, a door as wide again! It'll mean some stonework to make the opening a lot bigger and that's not my job.' It was unlike him to admit that there was a job not his very own.

'Are you on a big job at the moment?' Robert asked.

'I've just come back from me holiday: a week in London!'

'Then you're not on a big job?'

'No, and I'd like to be back at Zoygate again . . . not that it's a big job fitting a double-door frame and new door, but it's fine up there in the wind and the rain!'

Jack Wither's car turned into the yard, and as his customer had not arrived Robert and Nesta saw him at once in his office. He was a little hurt that it was not he who had had the idea of making a double front door but he could not but agree it was a good one. He had enough oak left to make a similar door and, if Mr Escrick would like it, they could get on with it at once, while the weather was good.

Robert would very much like it; as far as he was concerned they could start straightaway. He was reminded by Jack Wither that it would mean he had an untidy gash in the wall for several days, until the stonework was dealt with; all the more reason, he said, that they should get on with it quickly.

Driving back, Nesta appeared worried about the arrangements; she did not like the idea of the hole in the wall carelessly boarded up for a few nights, by which anyone who wished could get in easily; bent on robbery or worse.

How did she mean, worse?

Well, she meant that if anyone were in the act of robbery, with Robert waking up and hearing him, catching him red-handed . . . a physical attack might follow.

Robert reminded her that her fears might have been justified in London but not down here.

'Don't you believe that! You can still almost see the old salt puffing peacefully at his pipe, leaning against his boat; a bit like the drawing you've seen me doing, but believe you me, that's only camouflage; the crab and lobster business is a cut-throat job these days; there have been wreckers and smugglers and pirates and the lot along this coast since time immemorial.'

'Diddicois?'

'Don't make me laugh. They sound fascinating with that name but they're simply third-class gipsies and gipsies would deny they are of their ilk at all! And, Robert, it's terrible here in the winter; up at Zoygate . . . well, all those crippled, crouching trees behind your house, bent double with the storms. Grim and grey and icy. How are you going to stick it?'

'Go on about who is going to break in while I have a barrier instead of a door . . .'

'Well . . . as long as you realize that there are people about at nights, all night at this time of the year, and with no door there will be no security.'

There was a long pause and then she said, or even stammered: 'There's my cottage on the harbour at Carrioth; the sea just doesn't come up to there except in the worst possible weather; I sometimes have to put up overflow guests from the pub round the corner . . .'

She faltered because Robert had stopped the car and turned to look at her. She flushed and said, after a short pause, 'I have to go up to London soon to see my mother and father, as I told you. I go for at least a week every month. I'm very fond of them, they live in a flat in Holland Park. I mean, if we knew when the chaps were coming to do the stonework on your front door I could go just then and you could use my cottage.'

So the air cleared and Robert thanked her and said he would think about that but the nuisance was he had no telephone, so he could not ask the builders to ring him when they intended to call.

'I could do that for you.'

He had re-started the engine and she looked at him sharply: 'Why no telephone?'

'I thought I would not need one. I'm tired of telephones.'

She waited for explanation.

He said: 'There are things you think about when you are going to live somewhere you very much want to live, and these things you manage to achieve with luck . . . but there are a great many other things you miss out on.'

'Such as a telephone and . . . ?'

'I keep on realizing the rest.'

Most people would find it difficult to keep up a lively conversation for any length of time with someone they had just met and liked without mentioning anything personal. If he had done so, he had no doubt that she, too, would at least talk a little about personal things, such as she had just done about her mother and father.

It was not that Robert wished very much not to talk about himself, it was that for some curious reason he could not bring himself to do so; he now had a mental block about anything that applied to the day he arrived nine weeks before, and backwards from there to his cradle. She would have to take him as he was, with no background whatever, nobody who belonged to him or to whom he belonged.

So they continued to talk about the horrors of the present day, or about favourite pictures, or books, or things to eat, or what was going to happen next in these uncertain times. And when they had eaten some West Country cheese and drunk a bottle of white wine, she got up to go home, and he walked back across the sands with her and saw her cottage in the harbour with the harbour wall a few feet from her front door, across the road.

She had the sense not to ask him in at this juncture, and as he walked away he turned and waved and he saw that she was standing still and had not gone into her cottage but was waving to him.

And when he got back it was dark; he lighted a candle and put some writing paper on the table; he fetched his pen and wrote: 'Dear Angela . . .' but the words with which he had recently planned to start had gone and he was further away from it than ever.

'You will be pleased to hear,' Roundstone remarked, 'that the mermaid has been forbidden to come an inch further along the beach than the first breakwater.'

'It doesn't interest me in the least.'

'Well, it interests the police; it seems she has been watched a bit.'

'Why?'

'She must be keen on you.' Roundstone fell about with laughter which Robert did not share. 'For God's sake!' he exclaimed, looking disgusted.

Then Roundstone talked about the work to the frontage; he said he admired the way Robert put up with the people who would come to picnic at the weekends.

Robert said he did not put up with them, he simply had to stick it since they were entitled to be there. Roundstone then said he could entertain them with his accordion if Robert liked.

'*If I liked*,' Robert repeated, aghast. 'What the hell do you think? Of course you're joking.' But Roundstone was only half joking. 'They must have background noise, today's people; they cannot function without what they call music in the background. Music! I ask you! I might as well give them something at least with a tune and not nearly so loud.'

'And what would *you* get out of this?'

'Ten p. in my sou'wester.'

'Be reasonable,' Robert begged. 'I have an open mind but obviously you can't do it when I'm there!'

'Why not?'

'It would be intolerable; we'd have other itinerant musicians and before long a crowd. Don't be an ass!'

Roundstone looked crestfallen.

'I might say you could do it on an afternoon when I'm not here but I'm always here because there's nobody to ask me to luncheon.'

Roundstone narrowed his eyes: 'Hasn't anyone called on you?'

'The police. The Parson. The mermaid. The rating officer. The artist called Nesta. And I am awaiting with breathless excitement the visit of the social worker called Mrs Clare. But she's probably put it off in fear of an assault upon her ... by me.'

'They will call soon,' Roundstone said comfortably. 'All this excitement about you being a rapist is a flash in the pan – you'll see. It will all die down and the message will get about that you're a gentleman recluse, a *scholar*. And you will have lots of friends and, in time, you will "know everybody". Very unlike me.'

'Who is they? *They* will call soon, you said.' Robert
looked curiously at him. He was not in fun now, there was
a pained look on his face, but Robert made no comment
because he felt he would at once be treated to picturesque
anecdotes of the 'being left in a font in Manchester'
kind.

Nesta was as good as her word. Every day Robert wished
she would come and would constantly let himself look
out of the window to see if she had come the cliff way, as
she did before. He would not let himself go to see her. One
of these damp fogs that had beshrouded his first days at
Zoygate for a week was now repeated; the fog horns
moaned and he could sometimes hear the hollow calling
of people to one another below on the sands. Nobody
picnicked on the cliff edge.

After a week, the first personal letter he had received
actually arrived in the letter-box at the gate. It was from
Nesta telling him that the men would come to extend the
entrance on Monday; the new oak door had been
finished to match the present door and the job should,
with any luck, be complete by Thursday evening. Since
this fog could go on for days she had decided it was a good
time to go to her relations in London and would leave her
cottage on Monday morning. She would make up a bed
for him and leave the key at the pub, the Shaven Crown.
She very much hoped he would see the sense of this
arrangement and hoped that she would see him when she
returned next weekend.

PS. And by the way, in the telephone call she had had
with the builders, Mr Jack Wither promised that the men
who had previously worked at Zoygate should be the
same ones to do this door job. Did he not agree that they
were honest and reliable? But no answer required.

Nobody within an area of ten miles round was surprised
when Biddy Hallow, on the following Wednesday morning, was found strangled on the stretch of sandhills on the
Carrioth side, half a mile or so from Zoygate. There were

those, indeed, who claimed that they had been expecting it.

Granny Hallow did not report that she was missing till early on Wednesday and the reason for this was not a happy one: during the summer Biddy frequently stayed out at night. When she was fifteen this was very serious indeed, and Granny nearly went off her head with noisy anxiety. Social worker after social worker worked on Biddy for years; they made no impression at all.

So then Granny had to take the police into her confidence and tell them that poor Biddy was 'not all there', which, of course, they had known from the days when she would cast all her coverings from the pram and insist on being pushed down the main street in icy gales with a bare bottom.

For the poor woman's peace of mind the police agreed that when Biddy was missing they would endeavour to find her without appearing to do so, so that the rest of the world would not know she had vanished. And it was possible that Granny Hallow believed this and could carry her head high among her neighbours who kindly allowed her to go on believing it. More often than not, it was not a case of 'finding' her, she simply returned. When questioned as to where she had been she would giggle and her eyes would slide sideways; she made no attempt to speak. Her shoes or slippers would often give away the knowledge that she had walked a long way, at least to the next village which was five miles inland.

The police had spent many hours over the years scouring the countryside and all the adjacent villages in search of Biddy; they were more relieved than concerned when her crippled and crumpled body was found. And it was found within an hour of the news striking Carrioth; all those who had not to go to work or school turned out in the damp fog, and finally it was three women from the Reverend Crester's Mothers' Union who finally came upon poor Biddy. They were so excited that they did not remember about leaving everything exactly as it was, but between them caught hold of the body and staggered, literally, through the few yards of soft sand on to the hard dry sand of the high-water mark and laid her there. Perhaps they believed that there might be some life left in the girl, but they were quickly disabused of that when they picked her up.

They stood guard over the body, they shouted through the fog, and not one of the three wished to go and fetch help because each wanted the kudos of being one of those who found her.

'Help, help!' they shouted and people came running from every direction. A medium-sized boy was the first upon the scene and he could not be prevented from leaning over the body for a closer examination. 'Her eyes are popping right out!' he screamed, to the distress of the three ladies whose find the body was. They snatched him away and told him to shut up or his ears would be boxed. But many people, running to the cries, heard what the boy had shouted and it was the horror whispered from mouth to mouth all that day.

Granny Hallow had been cooking Mrs and the Reverend Mr Crester's breakfast bacon and had been so affected by the news that the District Nurse, who fortunately had not started on her rounds, put her under sedation.

Who was the first to mention the newcomer to the cottage at Zoygate? There is no record of this. In the midst of all the fuss, as they milled about waiting for the police and an ambulance Mr Robert Escrick came out of the cottage in the harbour, shut the door and slipped the key in his pocket. He was followed, as always, by his black dog and as they walked away eastwards back to Zoygate he passed through the fog such a crowd as might be coming away from a football match.

'What's up?' he asked someone whom he had never seen before.

And this man, having no idea who Robert was, shouted excitedly that Biddy Hallow had been found strangled on the sandhills.

Thank God for that, was Robert's first thought, though

his second was of a more Christian spirit. Poor girl, but she was asking for it! And as he walked on, ignoring the people who kept looming up through the fog, he thought: And thank God I have an alibi this time.

I was elsewhere is an alibi and there cannot ever have been a word more fickle and unsound. However, for the present it gave immense comfort to Robert. *Alibi.* It was as though someone had presented him with a delightful rose for his buttonhole; he wore it jauntily.

Yesterday afternoon Messrs Brown & Bright had brought the beautiful new oak door, the same as the one he had had in place; the new frame had been fixed in the space made for it and this morning, with luck, the new door would be hung to fit against the one now in place again. Nesta, the artist, had been so right; she was a clever girl. She had recognized quickly what was wrong with the appearance of the elevation, as Jack Wither called it. Robert acknowledged himself to be, though an excellent manufacturer of machine tools, a bit dim as a man-in-the-street architect.

It was just after nine when he arrived home. Fred Bedfont and his boy-mate were working on the door which was now in place and opened inwards into the house, with wedges of wood beneath the bottom edge to keep it in place. Brown & Bright's lorry was there and two other men were stacking the bigger pieces of granite that had been taken out to make room for the other half-door. They had just about finished and were handling the brooms with which they were going to brush up the rubble.

After Fred Bedfont had pointed out certain things to Robert, to underline the excellence of his work, he said: 'I'll tell you what, sir. You're going to have the gales lashing themselves against these beautiful doors. They'll stand up to it, I grant you, but you're going to say next spring that you need a stone porch with an outer door and I'm going to agree with you, sir. West winds up here . . . you can't believe it. It held up a lot of work on this property, I can tell you, this spring!'

The trouble about Fred Bedfont was that, though an excellent worker, he talked too much; he would have had Robert standing about for half an hour or more, listening.

Robert went inside to get his breakfast.

It was embarrassing that there should be any workmen there when the police arrived; he hurried out to meet them and leaned over the little car to speak to them before either had got out. He asked if he might come down and see them; he knew, of course, that he would be expected to give an account of himself over the Biddy Hallow affair and this he would gladly do, but not here.

After a little consideration they agreed and he promised to be there, at the little police station in Carrioth, at three-thirty prompt, and as they turned their car, having agreed to three-thirty at the police station, Robert thought that by that time some pathologist would have decided at what time poor Biddy had met her death.

He did not lunch with any good appetite and the presence of the workmen was intolerably irritating. Leaving Banjo in charge, he drove down to Carrioth and did some necessary shopping before turning up at the police station at three-thirty exactly.

With what fine confidence he entered the police station. He was never again to be quite his tall confident self, walking with high-held handsome head and springing step. He was interviewed by plainclothes men, two crime squad whom he had never seen before.

There were three relevant nights, Monday, Tuesday and Wednesday.

There was also Thursday, last night in fact.

The harbour cottage of the girl artist, Nesta, had been at his disposal for those four nights; she was returning from London on Friday or Saturday. He was to occupy the cottage every night during the period that the door of the Zoygate house would be simply boarded up, not securely but enough to give a sort of protection to the place.

The new doors were now fixed and he, having been home this morning, and inspected the progress of the work, intended, after this interview with the police, to go to the harbour cottage, pick up his night things, take the key to the pub, as arranged, and return to Zoygate. Thus he would be able to lock and bolt his new double front door before retiring for the night.

To sum up: on Monday he had gone down to the cottage on the harbour at ten o'clock, using the Range Rover, spending the night in the cottage with the Range Rover parked outside, and returning to his cottage at 9 a.m. where the workmen were bashing down the stone on one side of the door-opening to enlarge it.

Next night, Tuesday, he and his dog walked down to the harbour cottage as it was foggy, leaving the car locked at Zoygate. They walked back in the morning at 9 a.m., thus twice passing near where the corpse lay.

And last night . . . the same thing. This morning on returning to Zoygate, they had found the new door in place and by this present evening, he would be able to shut and lock it securely before going to bed.

So his alibi was, in his opinion, absolutely perfect.

Except . . . *except* that the examination of the body showed that it had been dead about twenty hours. There is always an element of doubt as to the exact time of death, depending on various conditions, weather, state of health of the deceased, time of year, whether killed indoors or in the open air, temperature of surroundings. These conditions are all considered with care.

So Robert's alibi, as he had almost affectionately been calling it in his mind, melted *into air, into thin air*. Instead of being a perfectly simple and straightforward murder on the beach, it became a hideously complicated and inexplicable event, as far as he was concerned.

Biddy could have been, and probably was, murdered at lunch-time on Tuesday and the shock of this news caused Robert to have an almost complete mental block about what he did yesterday at all. The days slipped by, eventless almost; one day Roundstone would be flailing the brushwood in front of the cottage; a letter was in the letter-box up the approach track one day; another day

he could not get *The Times* because they were sold out;
and yet another day there was a family of about eleven
picnicking before his eyes, and yet . . . there was this
obliterating fog. There was no incident or circumstance
which came to him so that he could definitely say something like: on Tuesday I was at home all day, there was a
thick fog. Perhaps he could, given time, but now, sitting
facing these two expressionless faces at the police station,
his mind was an almost complete blank about his movements until evening, when he was perfectly clear about
driving or walking to the cottage on the harbour. The only
thing he could remember with certainty was that he had
not seen Biddy Hallow at all, nor had he set a finger upon
her.

But when was the last time he saw Biddy Hallow?
He even forgot that.

'I . . .', He paused. The two in front of him were
absolutely motionless, not an eyelid flickered. 'I sometimes see her on the beach, fishing about under seaweed
growing over rocks. She feels about for unusual shells. I
never go anywhere near her.' And then he remembered:
the day Banjo played her up and she had hysterics. He
told them about the ghastly little scene. They knew
already.

They said they were taking the fingerprints of every
male person in the village and others within a certain
radius, and they asked for his. The fingerprint man from
the police headquarters took them. But everyone was
sceptical about this because only on the basket of shells
and shell trinkets and on the basket itself could a finger
imprint show, but Sergeant Crum remembered she had
been wearing a plastic belt and plastic slippers. But
anyway the basket had gone.

His confusion of mind was bad but in the higher regions
of serious thought there was still a clarity which allowed
Robert to approve of what was happening to him. He felt
a strong pride that at a time when society was riven with
hideous civilization-maiming crimes, two of the police
force's best brains were given to solving the problem of the

H

death by manual strangulation of an entirely valueless and redundant member of that society. He thought: Not a sparrow falls . . . But still, he was madly annoyed. With himself.

CHAPTER X

THE MORE he thought about it the more he realized that anyone from anywhere could have strangled Biddy Hallow. A lone cyclist enjoying a holiday in Cornwall; a man wandering off from a bus load of others stopping for a couple of hours for lunch. As Robert was only too aware, Biddy was an extremely irritating creature with her wandering fingers, her intense and ever present absorption with sex; she was like the poor man's Saturday night with the nudies, all for free. It was only too easy to imagine the mental state of the man who might ravage her, for ravaged she had been, and, within a few seconds, loathe her to the extent of strangling her.

He also thought that nobody within a radius of ten miles would have strangled her because all the men in that rather scarcely inhabited land's end would have either had her already or emphatically not had her, and would in either case therefore have lost interest.

So he was going to be left for the rest of his life with the finger of suspicion pointing at him: 'Look, he's the one who strangled poor Biddy Hallow.' Had he to live with this? Or would he have to keep a constant watch, a do-it-yourself detective, a kind of fifth-rate amateur, elderly detective (unlike Lord Peter Wimsey), on the look-out for the one who done it, for ever?

It was intolerable.

Friday; she was coming back today; within minutes of her return she would have heard the news from a village stricken but also intensely excited by the event. Would she come and see him tomorrow or wait till Sunday . . . or perhaps not come at all?

Or would she come this evening?

Roundstone came. He had finished the clearing job and they had had a great bonfire on the cliff edge. He made a discussion about what they should plant now on the bare piece of land the excuse for coming. He had heard about Biddy even sooner than Robert. He bounded up, anxious as everybody else to discuss the murder, but Robert silenced him with a look because there were still workmen around; not the ones who had fixed the new door but a stonemason who was doing the last fragment of pointing.

Come to think about it: what of Roundstone himself? A mystery man if ever there was one; he had declared himself to like the girl Biddy, Robert remembered, even praising her more than once.

'There's very little you can plant up here,' Roundstone was saying; 'nothing can grow if it doesn't get a chance. Azaleas and rhododendrons wouldn't have a hope.'

'Good gracious, man, I couldn't have rhododendrons blocking my view of the sea. I like it. I want to look at it all day.'

'Unfortunately you can't see it half the year, like today, for instance. What an opportunity to strangle a girl, if you happen to want to! I bet whoever did it hadn't any intention but did it only because he had the opportunity. Eh! Agreed?'

'I don't know,' Robert said irritably. 'Do you ever go to the pub down there in Carrioth?'

'The Shaven Crown? Yes, I do. It's a bit scruffy but it's all we've got and it was a lot scruffier when I first came here. There's been a new landlord recently; he has smartened it up a lot.'

'I've been in once or twice. I've wondered what sort of people go; they have residents.'

'Everybody goes, everybody, but not many residents; they've only got four bedrooms in all.'

'The types . . . I can't make up my mind. In the bar there's the fishermen and the land workers; in the snug, well, there's the odd smart salesman on his own and there's others I can't place at all.'

'What sort?'

'That's what I'm wondering.'

Roundstone looked across to make sure that they were not overheard. 'I see what you're getting at. You're asking yourself whether a visitor did for Biddy.'

'That's about it,' Robert said heavily. 'You see, my dear chap, there's no doubt in anybody's mind that it was I.'

'Yes, I've heard that one. It's village lore. Take no notice . . .'

'That's all very well . . .'

'The Shaven Crown,' Roundstone muttered. 'That's a curious name if ever there was one, isn't it? All the time I've been here I've been waiting for the legend that must go with it, and nobody's been able to tell me a thing.'

'What sort of thing do you expect to be told?'

'Some ancient monk or hermit . . .'

'The monk who raped the mermaid, sort of thing?'

'There's lots of grimy shiver-making tales around this coast, I can tell you! There aren't so many wrecks now as there used to be but over the past two hundred years, since the start of the Industrial Revolution, there've been some shocking bad wrecks. After a bad storm you'd find arms and legs and much worse. There was an old parson who made it his task in life to bury decently in the church-yard all the pieces of shipwrecked mariners that were found.'

The last two lorry workmen had cleared up and were now waiting to ask Robert if everything was satisfactory. Robert and Roundstone inspected the now double doors carefully and Roundstone was full of praise. 'It was the girl Nesta who is responsible, and it was Fred Bedfont and his mate Billy who put in the new door. It didn't take long!'

And as the lorry bumped and rolled away up the rough track Robert said it was only teatime but let them have some whisky; this immovable pall of fog was getting on his nerves. 'Of course it will move but it gives you the feeling that it is here to say. What *makes* it move?'

'Whisky,' Roundstone said. 'Enough of it makes such strong fumes, it gradually lifts.'

There was some reason for Robert's questions about the people whom he had seen this particular week in the Shaven Crown. They did not belong to Carrioth or, for that matter, to any Cornish seaside pub and they had looked as though they felt they did not. Robert had been sensitive to this. He had, in fact, run out of his store of whisky and this week, while Nesta had been away and he could barely see across the road for fog, he had been three times to the pub, this morning being the last time. Each time the three men had sat in the same positions, waiting. Two of them Robert had seen on the beach and overheard the conversation regarding Roundstone's boat. He remembered that he had thought them coastguards.

Waiting for what?

For the fog to lift.

So that they could take a boat out fishing?

Exactly.

But they did not speak much either to one another or to anyone else.

And they looked . . . well, they looked different. They sat stolidly drinking, reading the papers, then throwing them aside, lacking in animation and hard to stir at a time when everyone was milling around with their own particular Biddy-comment. Reports of what the police had done, had said, what they might do, what they said they were going to do next, what they might not do, how the present two imports were doing, what they had done and said, who they questioned, what the questioned ones answered or did not answer; it was a topic rich with speculation and endless guessing, exaggeration, or just plain lying.

Neither all this nor the amount of various drinks they were absorbing had the slightest visual effect. There they sat.

Getting a second drink for himself Robert had whispered to the girl who took the place of the landlord and his wife during the midday dinner period: 'Who are those three?'

'Strangers,' she said. 'They're waiting for the fog to rise, they've got a boat.'

'Where is it?'

'*I* dunno!'

And Robert sighed, thinking that it was sad when the young were found to lack curiosity.

'In the winter,' an old fisherman had told him, 'the fog sits over we for weeks betimes. Other times we're blown out of us beds with the wind; tears the skin off of we, it does. It's not a place to *live* in.'

It did seem that Robert's choice of a place to which to flee from the horrors of the present day was vicarious and not for him.

But walking back home across the sands Robert's thoughts had returned to the Three Men. Did they have a boat, and if so . . . what for? Certainly not for pleasure. Their clothes were those of people who ring at your front door with printed tracts, telling you to 'Smile – God loves you.' Good honest sober garments for concealing, but not for enhancing in any way at all.

Roundstone said that the good Robert was becoming as parochial 'as the rest of us'. 'What does it matter who the three men are? You should never have come here, man. There's nothing for you to use your brain about. Three men in a pub, tcha!'

'If you *don't* think and wonder about things round you, your brain goes to pot pretty soon, I can tell you. One of them might be the Biddy-killer.'

'You're a strange chap, Robert whoever-you-are. Perhaps one of these days you'll tell me who and why you are and why you call yourself Escrick, because you don't kid me that that's your proper name!'

'I'm just as suspicious about Roundstone,' Robert said, and laughed.

'I'm suspicious about Roundstone, too, but I do know I was called that shortly after my birth so I'm hardly likely to have it changed before I finally shuffle off.'

And I, Robert thought, shall I ever be Cravenhead

again? It was a good name, a name which bore with it
some credence. A name which gave people to think again
so they might shake their heads in some surprise that the
strangler of a half-witted mermaid upon a sea-shore
should really be a Cravenhead; a Cravenhead could
slaughter with the best in a war, but not that kind of
secret strangling in a fog, for him.

And while they drank, a wind started to whistle, a
slight sound at first, mounting slowly until the fog was
being blown away as though by an electric fan. Quickly,
quickly it disappeared and Roundstone, looking back
over his shoulder out of the window, gave a cry of pleasure
and jumped up, shaking himself like a dog.

'We're off,' he cried, 'we're off. Ta ta, friend, and thanks
for the drinks.'

He was, indeed, off down the path. And when Robert
had had his supper and cleared up he looked out and
there was the little red sail being blown out into the
sunset.

And Robert walked to the edge and looked, not at the
red sail, but back along towards Carrioth. He did not
expect to see anyone . . .

She was hurrying towards him across the sands.

He waved and she waved back and his heart was
bursting because he liked her very much; *love* had become
a suspect word but he did care whether he was liked or
not. To be liked was enough for the present.

But Nesta's face was sober, she clutched Robert's arm.

'What on earth has been happening?'

'Well, you will have heard. Poor Biddy Hallow has had
it and only half a mile from here. Last time she came to see
me she was on a donkey and it created quite a sensation,
you may remember. She brought her basket of shells and
shell boxes and tried to sell me something.'

'Yes, I know all that. And now there is an outcry for
the shell basket; anyone finding it has to take it to the
police.'

'For fingerprints.'

'Surely not!'

She stood looking thoughtfully at the new doors.
'Successful?'

'In appearance, very, very successful. You are a clever
girl. They have been quick about it, haven't they? They
were making the new half last week in the shop but the
whole operation here, breaking down the opening and all
that, *and* clearing away has taken a complete week.'

'You had the chap Fred Bedfont?'

'And his school-leaver assistant with the motor-cycle
and there were two others to do the stonework. Look!
That's the amount of granite they took out. It seems a lot,
doesn't it?'

They went inside and Robert prepared two drinks.

'But Robert . . . ?'

'Yes?'

'They've taken your fingerprints.'

'Yes, every male in the village under about eighty.'

'And over . . . ?'

'I don't know about that, certainly the over tens.'

'But Robert . . . ?'

'Yes, Nesta, what are you worrying about?'

'Lots of things; but why take fingerprints? Where do
they expect to find them? Fingerprints don't show on
clothes, not yet, though I believe they are working on it so
that soon finger marks *will* show on clothes, but not yet.'

'She wore a plastic belt.'

'But Robert . . . I hate to worry you like this but I feel
you ought to know. The whole village is taking it for
granted that you strangled Biddy Hallow; it's enough to
drive both of us potty!'

'Why you?'

'Because . . . because I happen to be fond of you.'

Speechless, Robert stared at her. He could not look
away from her.

She fidgeted. 'Don't look at me like that. I can't . . . I
can't help it.'

'Help what?'

'Liking you; even though I do not know the least thing

about you. Robert you have never told me anything but I
know, I absolutely *know* without a shadow of doubt, that
you aren't a criminal of any kind.'

'How do you know?'

'What a silly question. I just know, that's all, Robert
Escrick.'

The way in which she was looking at him made it almost
imperative for him to say: No, Robert Escrick Cravenhead, but he forced himself not to do so.

'I don't even know your full name,' he said instead.

'I'm Nesta Clare.'

'Hell!' Robert banged down his glass upon the table
and stared at her in horror. 'Not the Parson's social
worker?'

'Yes, as a matter of fact.'

'Well, I'm damned! He said he was going to send you.'

'But Robert . . . before I married I worked in welfare.
I was only married a year, then my husband was killed in a
plane accident about nine years ago. Only his mother was
alive and since then she has died and their money and flat
in London and cottage in the harbour here – well, it all
came to me. So I put my parents into the London flat,
which they love, and I used to live there with them because
I happen to like my parents, and then I realized I could
do what I'd always wanted to do and that was paint and
draw. I know I'm not much good but I like doing it. As a
matter of fact – ' and she tried not to smile – 'I sometimes
sell a picture, and did sell two this week. But that's by the
way. Well, I can't paint always, all the time, of course,
the weather is beastly a lot of the time, specially in winter.
So I . . . I offered myself to the Probationary Service here!'

'Good Lord!'

'Well, obviously someone of my age, thirty in March,
can't just sit around doing nothing for anyone but themselves for the rest of their lives. So . . . I offered myself to
the Probationary Service, and as I rather like kids and
haven't any of my own, I'm relegated most of the time to
what they call "disadvantaged" children, horrible word

but it sounds polite. I do it on a part-time basis down here in Cornwall so that I can go and stay with the aged parents when I want to, and paint when I want to, if suitable weather.'

'Have you a Mini?'

She nodded, but smiling. 'The Parson's such an old twit. He told me he had told you he would ask me to call. I can't imagine anything that would annoy you more. But since you seemed to be rapidly making your name as a first-class criminal I thought I owed it to you . . .' She stumbled about in words. 'I mean . . . what do I mean? I thought, perhaps . . . you might need some sort of help!'

'What sort?'

'Well . . . if only to talk about it and I knew you would damn well not talk about it if I arrived as a social worker. So I came just as myself . . .' she tailed off rather pathetically.

Robert was still scowling but it was relaxing a little.

'So, Robert, I think I can help a bit. I can't quite sort out my thoughts at the moment. But as I've been doing this quite a time, I have got to know a great many people all over the county, rather intimately. I might, I just conceivably might, be able to pick out a likely murderer of Biddy Hallow. And I know a lot about Biddy.' There was a long pause and she added: 'And I know a lot about Roundstone, too.'

Robert started visibly. 'Hell, I can't believe he comes into this.' She said nothing but put both elbows on the table, her face in her hands, and looked at Robert fixedly. 'In time,' she said, 'that is if you've got any sense at all, you get a feeling about people, whether they are genuine, or whether they are lying when they tell you whole long rigmaroles about how they have been misunderstood. A grievance. Nearly all the disadvantaged have a grievance. Have you a grievance?'

'By God, have I not!'

She smiled a little: 'You see?'

'Has Roundstone a grievance?'

'His is gigantic, absolutely enormous! Don't let's talk

about him. Anything I may know about Roundstone
comes from having heard him talk. He's not getting the
social worker treatment, you may be perfectly satisfied
about that. I've known him for years. I use the Shaven
Crown almost daily to fetch stout for myself and other
drinks when friends come. I'm in and out of it like an
habitual drinker, but I'm not that. It's fun to see who is
there and what visitors are around; it's a microcosm of the
community; in the summer lots of foreigners come just to
see what it is like.'

She ruffled up her hair: 'And so, Robert . . .?'

'I'm compelled to talk a bit about myself over this
Biddy Hallow affair. It amazes me that I should have
been picked out . . .'

'It is not amazing at all. The first night you arrived the
trouble with Biddy started in a big way. Nobody had
seen you or knew your name or anything about you,
except that you were a newcomer. It was perfectly natural
that you were condemned from the start.'

'What about Roundstone? Could he not be a suspect?'

'There's a difference: they are *used* to Roundstone.
They are certainly not *used* to you. You surely don't think
of Roundstone over this Biddy murder, do you?'

'I have done so.'

'Well, don't, for Heaven's sake. The very last man to
suspect. Roundstone's problems are not women. And
now I must go and get on with it.'

'I shall take you home in the car, it's getting dark . . . I
cannot have you wandering back home along the shore,
though the tide is nearly in!'

On the way back to Carrioth it was too dark for him
to be able to glance quickly at her face, so that he could
not see how she was taking it, and he told her: 'The
trouble is, I am not good at these questioning interviews
with the police, not at all good, but yesterday I really
made a fool of myself when they were interviewing everybody and I asked to go to the little local police station and
take my turn. It never struck me for a moment that the

murder was not done at night. I was so pleased with myself that I had no doubt whatever where I was during those four nights – at your cottage. I was thrown when I heard that it had happened about midday, twenty hours before the body was found. I simply could not, for several minutes, remember what I did during those days *at all*. In that obliterating fog or sea mist or whatever it's called, my mind must have been pretty blank; all I could remember was that I was reading somebody's diaries. They even wanted to know what diaries I was reading and I said *Chips*, which caused them to exchange the strangest looks. If they do not think I am a vicious murderer they certainly think I am the mindless sort, wandering aimlessly about the sea-shore, strangling the tiresome Biddy as aimlessly as I would eat a bag of chips.'

'You don't eat chips aimlessly,' she murmured, but very sober. 'Go on.'

'There's not really much to tell. It's not much, I know, but it's important because I do not want to go to Broadmoor, which, of course, it will be for an absent-minded dotty old creature of fifty-nine. At any moment now I will be ringing up my wife from the telephone-box in the village to say, "I'm in Carrioth, where should I be?" The answer is clear.' And Robert gave a nervous laugh.

There was now an atmosphere that he could cut with a knife. How was it possible to have said it: *my wife*.

There was long, palpable silence, or at least it seemed so to the guilty one. Thirty-five years of being married and that word *wife* had become taboo ten weeks or so ago; it slipped out without a thought.

But did the girl sitting beside him care in the least whether he had a wife or not?

All women do, they want to know within seconds of meeting whether you are married or not.

All women?

Perhaps not *all*. Perhaps not this girl Nesta whom he had discovered he liked very much. Perhaps Nesta would be affronted to think that he thought she cared whether he had a wife or not.

Nesta was an attractive, vivid girl with style.

But so was Angela.

Nesta was clever and gay and kind and greedy about food.

But so was Angela. She was all these things and beautiful as well.

The difference was that he was finished with Angela. He no longer loved her. That must be why he left her.

He had just started with Nesta but he liked her completely so perhaps he really was mad and he might well have strangled the unfortunate Biddy because she was neither Angela nor Nesta. *And there is nothing left remarkable beneath the visiting moon.*

Nesta said: 'I may not see you for a few days, Robert, because I am going to do a bit of research on my own, and by that I don't mean necessarily alone but I mean without any police assistance. I haven't worked in the villages round these years for absolutely nothing, I hope. I know them all. So good night, dear friend.' She squeezed his nearest hand to her and left him as she jumped from the Rover's steep step and ran into her own door, turning on the light inside at once and waving back to him.

CHAPTER XI

ON TUESDAY a Coroner's Enquiry was held in the stuffy little Church Hall. Robert had been certain that he would be called to give evidence, but on thinking it over in the cool of several days after the body was found, he asked himself what evidence there was against him beyond the happening in his bathroom on the day he had arrived, which latter was not at present relevant to the case now being investigated but would of course be considered later. His stumbling answers on the question of his alibi did not, when considering the whole matter, prove anything. The confident answers given by any suspect might, in fact, tell against such suspect considerably.

At the enquiry, evidence was given first of identification and then the police surgeon's report of the findings at the post mortem and there was some unpleasant discussion about the tiresome unclarified question of rape which the Coroner treated evasively.

Later, Biddy Hallow's uncle, described as Farmer Hallow of Edge Farm, stood up as a witness and said that he was responsible for the girl, having taken charge of her as a 'disadvantaged child' fifteen years ago (when that ungainly word was not used in the context). Both the girl's parents were dead, she had no brothers and sisters and his mother, Mrs Hallow, who worked at the Parsonage, had the girl living with her in her cottage in the village. She was not considered capable, he said, of doing any real work but she busied herself most of the time collecting shells with which she made trinkets and match-boxes which she sold occasionally, mostly to visitors in the summer months.

There was a long pause while the Coroner was obviously choosing the words with which he was going to enquire into the question of sex experience, but Farmer Hallow helped him out of the embarrassing situation by saying in a loud voice: 'She was not an experienced prostitute by any means, poor girl. She was just a clammy sex-pot!' Most people in the court kept their heads lowered in case they should catch the eye of someone thinking the same thoughts and laugh. Clammy sex-pot was so apt in the case of poor Biddy with her wandering clammy hands, seeking, clinging and clutching, and there were those who wondered how her uncle had the courage to so aptly describe her. No suspect was called, and the inquest ended with the Coroner saying that he would send the case of suspected wilful murder to the Director of Public Prosecutions.

Robert went into the pub partly for refreshment and partly in order that he could overhear any comments on the inquest from any customer who had been there.

Several people he had seen there came in and mostly ordered a pint of bitter, but there was a conspiracy of silence, or else no one had yet made up their minds.

The Three Men came in but not looking quite as they had looked last time Robert had seen them. Today they had discarded their town clothes and were muffled to the ears in polo-necked sweaters of a thick so-called fisherman's knit, and they were perturbed about, apparently, the misbehaviour of their boat. They spoke excitedly in Scottish or Irish accents and Robert could not make out all they were saying; an evident engineer joined them, his face smudged with oil and black oil on his hands; he had a mug of stout and an argumentative manner which increased as he drained the mug. At one moment Robert caught: 'Well, what can you expect if you hire a craft of that ilk?' and a little later on: 'You *were* warned.' Their heads together, their voices low, they thrashed out the situation. They all had a second round of drinks and came to some mutual conclusion; several place-names that Robert had not heard were mentioned. 'The goods' were mentioned several times, and Robert felt no doubt at all that they were smugglers. The one who was clearly in the middle of some job left them, flinging out as though he was annoyed.

Smuggle on, Robert thought, who am I to interfere with your affairs? He deplored himself, thinking of the self-satisfied retiring manufacturer of machine tools who had promised the chairman of his County Council that he would join the magistrates on the bench as soon as he had retired, and yet had no intentions at all of doing so.

These three were men with a mission; it was not for them to sit relaxed in a third-rate village pub, enjoying the local brew in pint mugs. If Robert knew anything about people, and he prided himself that he knew more about people than machine tools, having kept his employees happy and contented for forty years or so, not one of these dedicated men with a lot on their minds would have time for tackling Biddy Hallow, nor would seriousness of purpose be diverted into anything so entirely useless as strangling her. But then, of course, one can never be sure . . .

Robert, however, was sure on this frivolous issue of poor Biddy Hallow. He watched the second pint going down in the glass pint mugs, and when they were almost empty he strolled across the snug and offered them all another mugful. If they had only had one, they might have refused, but they had had two; therefore they accepted and they became relaxed, up to a point.

They had to have a valid reason for being there, of course, and none of them had the slightest doubt as to what it was: they were looking for a suitable site along the Cornish coast, both north and south, where they could get permission to start up a small boat-building concern. They had a successful small pleasure boat business outside Belfast, but owing to present circumstances, they needed to develop a concern where there were better prospects. The Government was taking a much greater interest in leisure for the people and these small thermo-plastic boats were likely to have quite big sales in a county that was crammed, in the season, with pleasure-seekers. These little boats were safer than houses, kids could play with them.

They took it in turn, as they pulled at their mugs, to allow bits of this information to drop out and Robert had the feeling that what was said had been rehearsed. It turned out that at present the boat in which they had come over from Ireland to explore the coast, was giving serious engine trouble, and in addition they had been unavoidably held up by the shockingly persistent sea mist that had hung about for nearly a week. And furthermore, the estuaries they wished to explore were not easy for those unfamiliar with the coastline. The one who seemed to be the leader of the party said that as far as he was concerned, an estuary for their workshop would be far more acceptable to the authorities who would have to give planning permission. The other two were not sure, they wanted to look carefully at the whole coastline for a small sheltered bay. At the moment they were stranded at

a small village on the east side of Carrioth and they were
employing a local engineer who seemed to know what he
was doing.

'The coastline is very far from being easy,' Robert said,
'it's bewildering. And from all round one hears about
the terrible weather. This corner of England really takes a
beating, from all accounts. You'd never keep a boat-
house building in an exposed spot for one winter, I'd say.'
But Robert had a strange feeling that they did not wish to
discuss it with him; they had enjoyed their third mug but
they did not want to go on talking about thermo-plastic
boats.

They turned their attention to the coastguard's station
and, not knowing much about it, Robert told them that he
lived in what used to be the old coastguard's station three
miles nearer Carrioth. One of them asked if there was a
constant watch at the new station; they believed not.
Robert said no, there was not, but he had not yet lived
here long enough to say what would happen in the rough
weather about which everyone had warned him.

A certain amount of exchanging looks with one another
now took place and one of them asked if trained coastguards were always used on their staff or whether local
untrained labour was sometimes employed. Robert
thought this an odd question; he did not give a straight
answer but asked if one of them were thinking of applying
for a job. He said this as though joking but their faces
remained remarkably unamused.

Since Robert was interested in the subject of Ireland and
its problems he sought to bring them out with a relevant
remark of no importance. They at once seemed to signal
to one another that it was time to be off. Thanking
Robert for his drink and implying that they had a lot to
do and would return the drink 'tomorrow, perhaps . . .',
they left.

The girl who was serving behind the bar winked at
Robert and shrugged her shoulders.

One or two of the locals were still sitting silently
around and Robert knew they were waiting for him to

I

leave, so, clicking his fingers to Banjo, who had been spending a boring morning waiting outside the church hall for his master and now in the pub, sprang to his feet and followed him. The locals exchanged knowing glances.

Nesta took out her big lined manuscript book in which she kept her own notes, observations, programme of work and details of the families which she called 'hers'.

She had nine 'problem' families, all her own business and all of whom she attended frequently, whether or not there had been anything new reported with regard to any of them. Only three of these had regular, properly married parents. Two had fathers in gaol, one had a father in a lunatic asylum (not to be called that under any circumstances), two had nominal parents, and the last was called a 'one parent' family. Thirteen couples of parents had, among them, twenty-five children; some of them were almost grown-up, school-leavers, and others had been established into jobs. The worst troubles at the moment came from the ten- to fourteen-year-olds and Nesta spent a lot of time simply listening. Listening to the complaints of parents against children, wives against husbands, children against parents, husbands against wives . . . it was all poured out. Often she heard the same words repeated to her twice or three times on one visit and all over again every time she called.

She knew the names of everyone on her list, of course.

After the first months of this work, which fascinated her up to a point, she did not really enjoy it. There was a dreadful similarity, fundamentally, in the problems, even though they might appear superficially to be excitingly different. Nevertheless, she had convinced herself that she ought to do this work for others, she rejected emphatically that she was a 'do-gooder', and trudged on without any conviction at all in her own methods or satisfaction in doing a job well. She was not even emotionally moved about Biddy Hallow, but she was deeply anxious about Robert Escrick. Anxious, yes, and angry at the stupidity

of the confirmed belief of everybody for miles round that
he was the culprit.

It would take about five days to interview her flock
properly. They were a scattered lot so she filled up with
petrol, took half a dozen bars of coconut ice from the
village sweet shop, and set off. She would be able to
return home in the evenings to a meal of fried or poached
fish, which someone would leave ready for her supper in
her kitchen every day.

There were fashions in misery and the present one was
'teacher-bashing'. Several teachers, ill-equipped for
strife, had left the schools and the classes were bigger than
ever and manned by those few teachers who were able to
overcome the disposition to fight off the leaders of the
packs.

In one of the districts Nesta had to visit on her second
day, the children had become so rough that two of them
had to be removed and, after consideration, a boy of
fourteen who was the undoubted ring-leader had to be
sent to a security unit. Nesta now referred to this one by
name because he had been so outstandingly the culprit in
leading the rest of the class into outright warfare when
one of the teachers had a severely damaged eye.

She asked the head teacher how Billy Bacup fared; it
was nearly three years since the trouble with him and
recently Nesta had written him off as having settled down
and he looked like becoming a responsible citizen with his
adolescent troubles behind him.

The teacher was enthusiastic, telling Nesta that Billy
was one of her successes, working now for a building firm
and nothing but praise from the foreman. 'You worked
hard on poor Billy, Mrs Clare. You deserve all the success
you have had,' the head teacher said.

Nesta glowed with pleasure as she drove away. Success
was the thing which made her work worth while. Billy
had been a particularly intractable child at first but she had
always liked him. In the long run he was so much easier
to deal with than some of the bigger children, who wore
sulky and suspicious expressions on their faces, discourag-

ing any approach or attempt to be friendly. Nesta could sometimes get through to them with the help of coconut ice but such success as she had was not lasting.

With the uplift she had just had about Billy, she approached the Bacup family more cheerfully than she usually did when visiting them at home. This 'home' was a council house that had been offered finally, as a last resort, to Mr and Mrs Bacup. They had lived for a long time in such squalor they were known as a 'problem family', and Nesta made a nuisance of herself, as she described it, for months trying to have them allocated a proper house. They were not gipsies nor diddicois and the father claimed unemployment money. Every job that had been found for him had occupied him for not more than two months; he did not leave of his own accord, the employees invariably begged to have him removed. He wore a puzzled look upon his wrinkled face as though he simply could not understand why he always got the sack. He had shown himself willing, indeed anxious, to be rendered sterile 'for the good of his country' so that he stopped at three children; but his country seemed unaware of the great sacrifice he had made and the rent collector's weekly visit was torture to everyone within hearing distance of the house and the people in the adjoining house had complained so bitterly about their neighbours that they were allowed a reduced rent as a solace.

They had so many possessions, mostly plastic, that the house overflowed and the space where others had a garden was littered with things that Mr Bacup brought back on a one-wheeled banana cart, like a flat wheelbarrow, from the town rubbish dump. His latest find was an abandoned electric washing-up machine and Mr Bacup gave every appearance of a man repairing it. Mrs Bacup also gave the appearance, at the kitchen sink, of a woman washing her children's clothes; in fact, neither of these things were happening.

'Now, dears, what's the latest?' Nesta greeted them cheerfully. She referred to the date of her last visit and asked about Maureen who, when she last came, was in

hospital with a ruptured appendix and the youngest
child, Gloria, had just fallen down some steps and broken
her front teeth; an ambulance had taken her to the
nearest hospital for dental attention.

After listening to some horrifying details regarding Mrs
Bacup's internal affairs, and a long dreary repetition of
the agonies Mr Bacup was suffering with his back, she
changed the subject from misery to good cheer and,
though she knew already that Billy was doing well, she
talked about him to cheer them up.

Yes, Billy was thriving, had bought himself a motor-
cycle and was living in rooms nearer his work, the owner
of which had a son who was a friend of his own age and
who worked in the same firm. He was looking forward to
the football season and in the meantime they played for
hours after tea, these light nights, with other football
enthusiasts in the village in which he lodged, which had
its own football ground, so called.

'. . . and there's no mucking about with dirty mucky
girls for our Billy!' Mr Bacup boasted.

This kind of work is not stimulating and by the end of
her working day Nesta was tired. It had not turned out a
nice day and it was now drizzling miserably so she did not
consider it a day wasted from art; nevertheless, she would
very much have liked to visit Robert Escrick but she had
told him she was working for several days and as she was
passing the gate at the end of Robert's track, where the
broken-down letter-box hung, she did not even slow
down. Much as she would have liked to call, she went
straight home to her cottage.

If she had visited Robert she would have found him
reading his *Times*. She would have observed that he read
it through to the Obituary Column which he sometimes
read carefully and sometimes not. This time his eye
glanced over the Personal Column and his own name
leaped out at him under Announcements.

SIR ROBERT CRAVENHEAD. A letter of some

importance is awaiting him in the offices
of Boston & Spar, Solicitors, at No. 90A
The Strand, London, W.C.

There was a lot to think about. Had one of the family
died? One of his grandchildren been killed riding his
bicycle along that dangerous main road? Had Angela got
cancer? Had the house been burned down?

If there was any serious trouble at the works, it was no
longer his concern. But if any of those family things had
happened he must return; sheer decency made it imperative. He would be a cold-blooded, heartless devil if he
failed to do that.

So how would he find out if any of these things had
happened? By telephone, of course, not to his house but to
the solicitors who had inserted the announcement. He
would have to ring Directory Enquiries for the number.
It was annoying that the solicitors had not put their telephone number but it had evidently been left out purposely.

His watch said five-thirty. It was too late to telephone
now, he would have to wait till morning because the
solicitor's office would be shut.

He went across to the window. It was raining quite
hard and up over the top came Roundstone. He often
thought of him as *old* Roundstone – he wondered why,
because if Roundstone was old, Robert Escrick was very
old Robert Escrick. He put the kettle on because under
the new anti-alcohol plan Roundstone would need a cup
of tea, not delicate china tea but a mug of tea made with
two tea-bags.

He flung open the new door and welcomed him in.
Roundstone was wearing a totally enveloping fisherman's
oilskin which he undid and dropped to the ground.
Robert brewed the tea and when his visitor had, sipping
appreciatively, approved of it, he sat down, his mind on
The Times, lying in front of him on the table. He sighed
because he very much wished he could discuss the
announcement upon which his eyes were resting at this

moment with his friend. How long would he be this secret and mysterious self that he had taken upon him?

Ten years hence would he be still in the same condition, making no real friends because he could never allow his friends into the secret of himself as Robert Escrick? He had complicated his own life immeasurably: there was always something he had to remember not to say, such as 'my wife', as he had said to Nesta only the other day.

These two people, Nesta and Roundstone, whom he was now pleased to call his friends, could never be real friends if they were never to know anything at all about Robert's life before they met him. How could they?

He thought: My friend, Robert Escrick who was . . . who is . . . whose wife . . . indeed, about whom one knows, in fact, nothing!

No, it would never work. And so far his experiment in living alone and anonymously had not been a success.

'What's up, old man?' Roundstone said, after he had done some very loud sipping from his mug.

Robert looked at *The Times* without picking it up; he was wearing his glasses and could read his own name on the back page, so large. It would have been so easy to show it to Roundstone, to tell him that he had un-accountably taken against his previous life and his wife and family, had 'escaped' to farthest Cornwall and now . . . look what!

'I think you are looking a bit off colour, my friend.'

'Me?'

Roundstone kicked his mackintosh irritably, his mouth organ fell out of the pocket and he picked it up and played, quietly and sadly, a Lament.

After a long pause he said: 'I think I ought to make a Will.'

Robert's eyebrows went up. It was about the last thing he might guess would come out of Roundstone's mouth. Perhaps it was the lament which caused it.

'Ye see, I've no folk and if anything should befall . . .'

'Have you been feeling ill?'

'No, no, not at all. But nobody knows at what hour one's end cometh.'

'Quite true.'

'Well, I've no folk, as I say, and I have some, well, some decent gear.'

'Really?'

'Well, there's my boat, I'd like you to have that, Robert.'

Robert was dumb; he could hardly thank him profusely.

'. . . and my accordion. And this mouth organ. And this oilskin. And there's one or two things in my cabin I'd have you keep. And – ' he fumbled about in his trouser pocket, bringing out the round stone he had told Robert had been left in the shawl which had covered him as an infant in the Manchester font. He held it flat on his palm and looked at it. 'A keepsake in memory of old Roundstone!'

'Do stop it,' Robert begged. 'You're pulling my leg.'

'I'm not pulling your leg,' Roundstone said sadly, his face like the map of Ireland itself. 'I've got enemies.'

'Haven't we all?'

'I guess you haven't any . . . not any who know you, only those who call you names – not knowing you from Adam!'

'Well, go on, tell me about your enemies.'

'It's when you have a cause, that's when you have enemies.'

'Yes, it is.'

'You know what my cause is, it's writ all over me, they say.'

'Ireland?'

'What else?'

'You should leave it alone. Ireland's been a cause for so long now, three or four hundred years and it's still with you. You *need* a cause, you Irish.'

'Hell!'

'Yes, you need a cause to . . . to make you what you are . . . otherwise, you'd just be . . .'

'Be what?'

'Damned dull, perhaps. No, I don't mean that. For God's sake don't let's talk about Ireland and causes.'

'I wouldn't if I didn't think I should make my Will. I don't want all my goods chucked about, owned by anybody. I want you to have them, if necessary, so I am going to buy a Will form when I'm next in Truro and you'll see!'

'Well, then, you'd better please take me out in your boat and show me the ropes, literally.'

Roundstone looked doubtful.

'If and when I inherit I shall look a real Charlie, struggling to get the sails up. I don't know a blessed thing about boats and messing about in them.'

Roundstone thought this over.

'Okeydoke, then. The next fine evening, or maybe the next fine, calm, soft evening but one. It needn't even be fine, but calm, so's you won't be sick!'

Robert found this concern for his very few possessions unbearably touching: there was something about the man . . . he was unable either to put a name to it, or to understand what it was.

CHAPTER XII

THE HARBOUR in Carrioth barely merited the name, so small was it, and there was a lot of grumbling among the natives when the crippled thirty-foot boat called the *Colleen Bawn* was being towed in and scraped its side in a long deep scratch along the corner of the jetty.

The sail having been useless in the sea mist, the ancient vessel, with its engine at full speed ahead, had puffed and groaned and creaked its way down the Irish Sea, through St George's Channel, and round the tip of England between Land's End and the Scilly Islands. The passengers (two) were landlubbers to a man; they knew a lot about explosives and nothing whatever about boats of any kind. They lied completely about the boat-business near Belfast. The experienced old sailor they had employed as the third man for the trip knew a lot about sailing but, as it turned out, not very much about the motor. He had not much of an idea what the trip was about because it was obvious, even to him, that it was not a pleasure trip. They were exploring the coast but not for the reasons they were handing out.

The passengers, both, had hired a car with which they had been exploring the coast for a fortnight now, and during that time the engine was supposed to have been put in order by a Belfast engineer, who, it was believed, knew everything there was to know about marine engines.

There was a packing case on board, pushed out of the way under cover in the prow, and there were sundry weapons in their cabins, stowed away for self-protection if necessary.

All this was now common knowledge, which had certainly not been intended. It was obvious that this was a project which had gone wrong and the easy explanation for it all, the seeking of a suitable place to build a boat shop, all too facile.

Roundstone had no car or vehicle of any kind other than his bicycle, but now he was well known in the district and if he wished he could always get a lift from one of the coastguards into the village of Carrioth. It so happened that on the day after the *Colleen Bawn* was invalided out and towed into Carrioth's small harbour, Roundstone came into the village with one of the coastguards and saw the monstrosity in the harbour, exclaiming with surprise. The coastguard knew all about it, of course. Three Irishmen exploring the coast for a place to make plastic pleasure boats for the new rich, he called them sourly. 'They're stuck with that old craft. She's only fit for the scrapyard.'

Roundstone took the coastguard into the Shaven Crown to give him a drink as thanks for running him into the village. The three Irishmen, ill-disguised as sailors or fishermen in their thick-knits, were there too because where else was there for them to go and what for them to do? They were sitting in the main bar because they seemed to fill up the snug intolerably; it was the landlord who suggested they move into the bar and since they were there now almost the whole of the evening and much of the day too, they sat, absorbing the stout in quantity and looking thoroughly put out.

It seemed now to have come to the pitch that they would have to abandon ship, leave it in the harbour at some expense and return whence they came by some other means.

Roundstone, as a regular customer, got this much out of them within the first few minutes; he also had suggestions as to who, among marine men in the district, it might be advantageous to call in before doing anything so unsatisfactory as leave the old wreck in the harbour even at a price, causing some annoyance to the locals. Discussion livened up; Roundstone told them of a man in a village ten miles away who was an excellent engineer and might be able to produce the necessary part or parts that needed replacing; he wrote out the name and telephone number, telling them to mention his name, the man knew him well.

This seemed to be the best bit of news they had had and soon it was decided that if this expert could be persuaded to come and his opinion sought, they should return to Belfast, leaving the one they called Con behind to look after the boat. Some customers in the bar, who had followed this discussion, started telling them the best and quickest and cheapest way to get back to Ireland by air.

Presently the conversation turned to the murder, as it had done so often in the past week. The Irish visitors had not shown much interest as yet, their own troubles apparently transcending the manual strangulation of a village maid, known by all. There was endless discussion regarding the inquest, something that did from time to time happen when a particularly bad storm had dashed a small boat to bits on the rocks and the bodies, or parts of bodies, had to come under the scrutiny of the coroner, and when the occasional visitor paid no attention to the frequent warnings of *Danger* and got himself accidentally drowned.

'She'd this basket of fancy goods she'd made from shells,' someone said. 'If anyone found that it'd be a help . . . can't be, surely, someone strangled her for the shell boxes she made?'

'You never know!' someone else said profoundly, 'You never know what folk get up to these days. It takes all sorts . . .'

And in the midst of all the talk Roundstone found himself staring at the man called Mac. It was not that he thought he had seen him before, or that he saw in him a possible murderer; it was that he did not think he was an Irishman, in fact, he was unmistakably a Scotsman and spoke with a strong Glasgow accent. He recognized the type – an Orangeman, and this one happened to have orange hair and an orange beard.

Roundstone moved nearer and looked carefully at all three of them, so carefully, in fact, that they were annoyed. 'You'll recognize us next time,' the one who was not Mac said.

'You're Orangemen, aren't you?' Roundstone remarked. What he wanted to say – Then you're no friends of mine – remained behind the barrier of his teeth but he turned, banged down his empty mug, nodded to a chum of his and walked out, looking as though he wished he had had the nerve to spit in their faces.

The man with the orange beard whistled through his teeth to draw the attention of the landlord. 'Who's that?' he asked the landlord, jerking his head in the direction of Roundstone's receding back.

'Chap called Mr Roundstone, works up at the coast-guard station.' The landlord was busy, he had no time to gossip. As he drew down the beer handle he looked straight at Mac. 'Irish. Chum o' yours?'

'No chum of mine!' Mac exclaimed, but the landlord

had filled the mug and was handing it to his customer, he did not pay attention.

But the barmaid did. 'Oh dear,' she squeaked. 'Mr Roundstone is a nice man, he comes in with fish for us, times.'

'Fisherman, is he?'

She nodded. 'He's a great fisherman; he's got that boat with the little red sail . . .'

'Come on, Aggie!' somebody roared. 'Hurry up, girl!'

She giggled off.

An old man standing close sidled up to the red-bearded Mac. 'What was that he called you?'

'Tch!' Mac emptied his mug and called for more.

'Orangemen, was it?' the old man hissed. 'What's them?'

'It's a political party, if you want to know.'

'Political party, eh?' the old man wondered.

With a freshly filled mug in his hand Mac was prepared to be amiable. 'Freemasons,' he said laconically.

'Oh, them!'

'Not the sort you mean. We're Protestants and we have been for centuries, well, two centuries . . .'

'You the sort that make all the trouble, eh?'

'Now, you shouldn't ought to have said that. You don't get me. We aren't IRA. Anyway, we're a secret society and I'm not telling you more.'

'Have you got it against young Mr Roundstone, then?'

'Young Roundstone!' the Scotty exclaimed. 'Is that what you call him?'

The old mischief-maker could not resist the attention that was being paid him by a stranger; nobody else ever listened when he spoke. 'What's the word they use, eh? An *unfrocked* priest, Mr Roundstone is, that's why he comes so often to the Shaven Crown. Not that I've got the slightest idea what *unfrocked* means, sounds like something more like happens to a woman if you ask me. But some of the old sailors call their jerseys frocks – can you beat it?' and he gave a long-drawn-out wheeze which was by way of a laugh. It went on and on and developed into a bad

fit of coughing during which the Irish-Scot watched him
with a kind of excited look on his face.

When the wheezing upset was over he beckoned with a
long finger. Together he and the old gossip moved out of
the push beside the bar, into a corner. 'Did you mean
that, what you said?'

'About the priest?' The old man nodded vigorously,
pleased to have attracted attention to the extent he had.
'He's been here years . . . years. When he first come, he was
looking for a job as gardener, he was working for the
squire before you could say knife. Went on for a coupla
years, so he did, and more.'

Thoroughly enjoying himself, the old man gave a good
pull at his mug of beer. 'It shocked the place when a bus
load of priests arrived . . .'

'Bus load!'

'Well . . . you know . . . in a big black car. Father
Jether, they wanted. Nobody knew who he was or where
or what. Father Jether! They put up here at the Shaven
Crown and ordered some grand food and they put a
notice in the window of the post office down there . . . it's
the ironmonger's too. This notice, it was four times the
size of the other threepenny notices, they paid for it
special . . . a big one, they wanted! *Will Father Jether
come to the Shaven Crown.*'

'And then . . .?'

'Well, we can only guess the rest. They came . . . they
stayed three nights, it was out of the tourist season. Mr
Roundstone was living in a tied cottage belonging to the
squire; they all went there. They shut the door and
windows and they talked and they talked, for days, well,
three days. And then they went, just like that, they
went.'

If the old man's newly found listener had not listened
with such acute interest, he would not have poured out all
this stale old story. But these days nobody listened to him,
and he could not resist the Irish-Scots' interest in his old
piece of history.

'What's your name?' his fascinated audience asked.

'Trevis, Jim Trevis, seventy last Sunday week. Postman at Carrioth these past fifty years and now an old age pensioner *if you please.* I dare say you think I'm a busybody . . . everyone in t'village does. But they come to me quick as anything if there's aught they want to know, bless me, they do.'

He put down his now empty mug and brought out his short pipe. 'We're not much of a post office these days eether, believe me,' he droned on. 'Nor a sub-post office, if you ask me. We don't even have the village name stamped on the letters, or the time posted or . . .'

But he was cut short.

'Tell me more about Father Jether. I'm interested. He's an Irishman like myself!'

'You Irish?' the old postman exclaimed. 'Bless me, you sound Scotch, to me. I've got a Scotch son-in-law talks just like you!'

'Never mind that, I'm Irish, born and bred.'

'Scotch dad, then . . .' he argued mildly.

'This Mr Roundstone or Father Jether . . .'

'What's making you so keen?' Trevis asked, looking at him under his bristling brows. 'Thinking he done this murder we're all talking about?' He gave another loud wheeze as he pressed the tobacco into his pipe. 'You're barking up the wrong tree, he's not that sort.'

'Oh, clever old man, you know the sort, do you?' Mac said bitingly.

'Mr Roundstone is . . . well . . . he's getting on for a gentleman.'

'What do you mean . . . getting on for?'

'That Mr Escrick, come to live here a few weeks ago, just left the pub . . . he's a gentleman, if you want to know. Now that gentleman . . .'

He was becoming diffuse and out of hand, there was no more relevant gossip forthcoming; he had spilt a considerable amount of beans for one pint of beer. Mac seemed to have decided to leave well alone for the time being. He rejoined his friends.

Heads together, they sat at a table away from the bar so

obviously that some of the customers were nudging one
another and winking: 'What are *they* up to, eh?'

'... unfrocked's the word,' Mac said, breathing heavily,
'and don't that mean expelled in the RC Church?
Expelled! Kicked out! Eh, how's that? Means he's penni-
less. Or do "unfrocked priests" go along to the Labour
Exchange and ask for a job?'

'Maybe they do,' one of the three put in.

'We can only go along ourselves and ask.'

'We can't do that! They'd never tell us anyway. "What
do you want to know for?" they'd say. No, it must mean
sacked! Unfrocked! It's the sort of rum expression they'd
have, those RCs, different from everybody else. Unfrocked!'

'And they have a Shaven Crown too,' the third discovered. He did not find it funny but spoke as though it
was just one more reason for extermination; disgust
crumpled his face.

'They probably shave their crowns so's a woman won't
look at them,' the golden-locked Mac put in. And after
he had recounted the whole conversation he had had with
the old postman, they considered the situation.

'There might be something in it and there might not.'

'How did he know the name . . . Jether.'

'We should leave no stone unturned, even a Roundstone,' the second put in without the spasm of a smile
crossing his face. 'If it's his, the little boat with the red
sail, then what's he up to?'

'Fishing?'

'Yes?'

'We've got to find out. We can't blow the wrong chap
into what he'd probably call Kingdom Come, without
being sure he's the damn spy we're looking for.'

'Let's face it, priests are clever, they're damned clever,
cleverer than us even. No, I mean it. Sly and . . . well,
they know what's what.'

'You mean . . . we don't?'

'I don't mean that at all. I mean, he's been here all
these years and I'll bet you a penny to a pound not a

single soul knows what he gets up to out there in his little boat. But if all that trouble we've had has been coming from a boat that size we needn't cut our own throats because our own *Colleen Bawn* has conked out, let us down or whatever.'

'It'll be bloody marvellous if we've really spotted our chap by accident, like. They won't believe it, back home. Father Jether . . .' he mused.

'I'm not sure if I believe it, right here. It's like you, Mac; you're the hell of a bloody optimist. Seven years this unfrocked joker's been calling himself Roundstone, directing all the bloody gun traffic from the East here, there and everywhere, like he had a special message from God to the IRA.'

'By God! There won't be a small piece left of him, if I have anything to do with it.'

'Yes, yes, agreed to all that but it's got to be the right man, Sandy, you'll be with me there. Otherwise we'll blow the whole show away: the Battle of the Boyne will look like a Sunday School outing.'

'Oh, come on! The first thing is, finding out if that boat we found when he was not using it, is really his. First things first. The boat will show something, you bet . . .'

'What about the tide, man?'

'The tide?' Mac repeated as though he had never heard of it.

'You know how it floods in . . . half a day could be lost. It floods right up inside some of these caves, and you bet he'll hide the boat at the top of one of them so nobody on foot or even swimming could reach it. You'd have to be a bloody good swimmer to carry on up the shore with the backwards pull this blessed coast has. I don't want any of us drowned, that wouldn't help anybody!'

Mac banged down his fist on the sturdy Britannia table and several people looked round: 'Come on out in the open where we can't be overheard!' And when they left they walked round the corner to the harbour and sat themselves on the wall, heads together.

Home from her work, Nesta saw them, straight across

K

the road from her cottage. A few yards further along their wounded boat was tied up and at that time of evening nobody was doing anything to it. They were sorting out their plans which, owing to circumstances, were turning out to be diffuse and indecisive. But not entirely unsuccessful. They had started out from Belfast with the idea of tracing, tracking down and destroying a body of IRA sympathizers who had, for the last six or so years, made it easy for the cargoes of explosives to travel westwards round the corner of England and then northwards to deliver their explosives at any one port along the whole coast of Eire that would be indicated as the suitable one for the operations planned on a particular occasion.

The explosives sent from America were dealt with by others and had nothing to do with the particular sources these three Northern Irelanders had set out to investigate in Cornwall. The loads that came down the English Channel and turned that corner to Eire came from the East, and in the past had been sent from various places to a variety of little ports in Eire, the names of which were numbered and in code, so that, at the actual time the vessel carrying the contraband explosives was turning the corner of England, the exact port where its arrival would be expected was indicated by a short-wave radio link. This had a range of about twenty-five miles at sea and worked on a fixed frequency outside the authorized bands normally used by ships and therefore unlikely to be detected by the shore stations.

It was sheer guesswork as to how many people were involved in this operation. An agent somewhere would have somehow to inform the operators which port was expecting delivery upon a particular night.

It sounded simple but, as one of them said, it was just about as easy as catching a grasshopper left-handed.

It was simple, all the same; given the know-how a little child could have done it. From the reports they received over the years from their spies about some of those tiny Irish seaside towns with landing facilities, there had never been a hitch, other than weather-wise, when, perhaps, a sudden storm would blow up and delay the actual landing.

But it was worrying this end. A fragment of gossip from the postman in an unimportant pub about a so-called 'unfrocked' priest, sent them into a spin of certainty that they had found those whom they were seeking.

But they were undecided about the manner of destroying the set-up. They had their case of home-made explosives ready to be put together on board the *Colleen Bawn*.

One of them had been lent a new kind of weapon supposed not yet to have been used in the war in Eire: part pistol, part machine-gun, a 9 mm weapon said to be well suited for undercover operations and issued to individuals rather than units. It was called a sub-machine-pistol.

The Ulsterman called Mac had been entrusted with this weapon about which he was not at all happy; and he kept it in a suitcase. It did not look efficient, just the sort of thing an Irishman from Southern Ireland would invent after a night out, he thought it. It looked like a pistol only at one end; the other end was more like a toasting fork, the centre an instrument for applying death to greenfly in a greenhouse. Apart from every other consideration, it was impossible to conceal it about the person. If he really intended to fire it, he would have to be damned sure he fired it at the right person, otherwise there might be a burst of scornful laughter from the undergrowth.

Nesta, sitting on a low chair just out of sight by an open ground-floor window, heard most of the foregoing, bore with them while talk of the kind drew them together and reminded her strongly of Three Bad Men plotting together in a comic strip which she happened to have noticed in her travels of the past four days. The wheeling seagulls, circling above, waiting for food to be thrown them, seemed to be mocking the worried looks and sobriety of the wall-squatters.

Roundstone was proud of his achievement 'for his country',

as he thought of it. Though on the whole he had done well at priory school, he had the great disadvantage of being bad at sums. Right from the start of his activities he had been warned that he must have a head for figures, but he had discovered in middle school life that he was innumerate. Since at the time he had disliked arithmetic so much, he made no attempt to conquer his disability.

Then, when he had returned to the secular world, he had offered his services to the Sinn Fein, telling them his history. It was a pity there was no one who could produce a written testimony for ex-Father Jether, but discreet enquiries were made over a period of two years and finally he had to return to Ireland to interview the Committee. He passed, with reservations: he must at least learn to remember numbers and to have them clear in his mind with no uncertainty whatever.

For six months Roundstone cut the rough turf at the coastguard's station and dug over the vegetable beds, a crumpled piece of paper with numbers on in his pocket from which he refreshed his memory from time to time. It was easier than listening to confession but more boring, often he would find himself muttering numbers as diligently as he said his rosary beads while thinking of something else. But in the end he knew the code number of every small port round the coast of Ireland that might be chosen upon a particular date for delivery of guns, ammunition and material for explosives of every sort.

There was a list of twenty-eight places where there were agents ready and able to carry out the unloading and distributing of the cargoes at a given time and they, too, were numbered.

By post Roundstone would receive a note with the name, the date and time of the passing of the vessel chosen for the operation from the agent in charge of the operations and the code number of the night landing area. He would make preparations and within three hours of the time planned for the operation he would ring the code number to find out if the weather was OK and the munitions actually on their way. This confirmed, he could make final preparations on his boat. Whether or not he took the sails was a matter of the wind. Having decided, he would make the usual preparations for a night's fishing trip: his big fishing basket and rod and such nets as he might choose. He had a grey metal box which he packed at the bottom of the bag carefully. This was a miniaturized transmitter/receiver, part of a short-wave radio link provided by the gun-runners. It had the aforementioned twenty-five-mile range.

The ships involved in this operation also had a transmitter/receiver installed which was switched on only when nearing, in this case, Land's End or any other contact area.

Roundstone was able to judge how far to take his boat out before he started the operations, and when this point was reached he connected the receiver to a car battery, normally kept in the boat to operate the mast-head light.

He assembled his fishing rod which was, in fact, a telescopic aerial. He connected it to a terminal on the grey box and switched on. He listened for the hum of the inverter. That working all right, he switched to *transmit* and checked his aerial current. If all was well, he switched off to conserve power until time to make contact.

The arranged contact time drawing near, he switched on to *transmit*. He gave the pre-arranged call sign and switched to *receive*. Everyone is always very polite on the air, often there are more *thank you*'s than there are other words in these messages. In a few minutes he heard the answering *thank you* distinctly, in spite of constant interference.

'Which number tonight – over?'

A quick flick of the switch to *transmit* and the cryptic message was passed, the number of the Irish harbour or jetty awaiting the ship's arrival – over – quickly to *received thank you*. Check number again. *Thank you.* Roundstone confirmed with *over and out*.

The gear was disconnected from the battery, the fishing rod-cum-aerial was dismantled, the grey metal box returned to the bottom of the fishing bag, and the important part of the night's work was done.

The boat was dealt with upon landing in accordance with the conditions of the sea and the tide, and over the years Roundstone had excelled in deciding what the conditions would turn out to be. So far he had never made a mistake, and he never took risks if there was a sign that the weather would change to stormy.

There was one more thing he had to do and that was to take his old bicycle from the shed where the grass-cutter was kept at the coastguard's station and ride two miles, mostly an uphill winding gradient, to the telephone-box to report that the operation had succeeded.

He would ride down the road on the way back, his hair blowing back, sometimes laughing like a wild seagull at the mouth of the cavern where he kept his boat dry and where the sea roared at high tide, and sometimes eldritch laughter.

CHAPTER XIII

ROBERT WAS deeply unhappy; he had had a good try at forgetting or pushing impatiently aside that advertisement in the Personal Column. All his life to date, he had never been worried about what was the Right Thing to Do. He had always known instinctively what he should do, and that he should have been considered a successful business-man who had not purchased his knighthood but won it in competition with other businessmen spoke, for itself.

Furthermore, he had succeeded in doing what he had planned to do about his retirement, alone. So far the actual planning had gone without a hitch. The fact that he did not wish anybody at all to know where he had gone was an idiosyncrasy which he was totally unable to explain. His actions would certainly have rendered a number of people pretty angry, grieved, puzzled and impatient.

Put simply, he could shout to his critics, *I need a period of absolute peace*. The answer could come: And have you succeeded in attaining absolute peace? No, he had not and he had realized that there is no peace this side of the grave. On the other side of the grave . . . total peace maybe, but not here on earth.

Thinking over his situation, as well he might, what had happened to him was sheer bad luck; to start his new life as one who rapes, known as such to everybody within a whole county, was, to put it mildly, a bad start.

In reasoned argument he put it to himself that if it had not been for the whole Biddy Hallow episode, up to the hellish finish, he would not have hesitated to answer the cry for him in the Personal Column of *The Times* at once. As it was . . . what a fool he was going to look! To have left his entourage when on the crest of the wave, last seen at a City luncheon on the day of his retirement and two and a half months later found cowering in a two-roomed converted coastguard's station on a cliff top in Cornwall, suspected by all the locals as a raping murderer, was quite intolerable.

And yet . . . he might be desperately needed by those whom he called his own, those whom he had loved and cherished, those of whom he had once been so proud . . .

'May I come in, Robert?'

Caught red-handed being sorry for himself, Robert could not answer. He could neither smile nor speak; he could only go to the drinks tray yet again and pour out a drink for Nesta and for himself. He handed the glass to her and raised his own glass to her, face stiff with misery, and a tiresome thing happened: his eyes filled with tears. Fortunately he was wearing his dark glasses. It was not self-pity which caused his eyes to fill, it was the sight of Nesta whom he liked so much that it must be love even though he denied it. He wanted never to have her out of his sight; to talk to her, to walk with her; to sleep with her, to drive in the car with her, to be with her every moment of his life; and yet how very far from it he was and the tears might well be tears of rage and frustration.

The Times was lying on the table, it was folded in half with the back page containing the Births and Deaths and the Personal Column face upwards; from where he sat, in his rocking-chair he could see his name: Sir Robert Cravenhead. He could so easily point to it and say: 'That's me.' And yet, he could not do it!

'Well, Robert,' Nesta said at last, 'don't talk to me if you don't feel like it, but I must talk to you.' She did not smoke but she put down her glass with a thump in the absence of a cigarette to press out. 'I've been seeing my families for the last four days, if you know what that means. I've got these problem families which I think of as all mine, I am responsible for them, and it does me a great deal of good to delve into their ugly disputes and controversies, even if I don't enjoy it, in fact I . . . no, I won't say it.'

She paused. 'But what I'm going to talk to you about is your – indeed, mine too – friend Roundstone. How curious, isn't it, that in nearly every house I have been to visit some one has mentioned "the wicked man" at Zoygate and who do you think they mean? You! It is utterly too absurd! You're simply a scapegoat! A vehicle of the troubles of others!

'And yet, Robert, where all the real trouble stems from is our mutual friend bloody Roundstone. Seven years . . . what shall I call it, consistent wrong-doing? It isn't a question of whose side you're on; whatever side you're on it's WRONG, WRONG, WRONG to blow people to bits. Well, to put it a bit more mildly, it's wrong to injure other people deliberately. This damned friend of ours, so full of himself and his mysterious virgin birth . . . oh no, that was last year's myth, this year it is a font with a marvellous lid, in Manchester! Roundstone and his damned mystery! He's just a hanger-on for the IRA. A hanger-on! He doesn't even risk his own life . . . much.'

She slumped for a long time in her chair, gently rocking. 'Hatred wears you out, doesn't it? As a matter of fact, I don't hate him. I like him, I can't help it, I like him with his accordion and his Irish tunes, and his . . . oh hell!'

There was a long pause during which Nesta felt desperation and Robert felt sad, but very sad.

'These three musketeers – no, bombardiers is the better name because their speciality is booby-trap bombs, that doesn't sound too bad, does it? It sounds more like a schoolboy bomb. Well, whatever it is called, it goes off with lethal effect. These bombardiers, Robert dear, are on their own, a dedicated band of brothers loyal to their six counties and determined to help with their own, their very own, spy system and dedicated sabotage of any and every attempt they can track down, to land explosives on the coasts of what they consider their own dear land. Indeed, they have been quite successful half-a-dozen times or so, but they are handicapped by having to, at the same time, earn their livings, and so their work against these illegal imports of explosives has to be done in their spare time and the present happens to be their three weeks' annual holiday and they have been in the course of planning it almost a year. Weather, too, has had to be considered and lack of funds. That's why this extra-ordinary vessel, the *Colleen Bawn*, bought from a scrapyard and patched up for this adventure, hasn't been a success, so far.

'Two of them are Scots by birth, and you don't have to listen too carefully to realize that! The third is, or sounds, pure Irish. The two are soaked in the fighting spirit of their ancestors, always roaring over the Scots border, waving their axes or their bows and arrows or whatever, and all on their diet of mealy puddings!'

'You're on their side, I see.'

'Why take sides? When all is said and done . . . WHY?'

'Because it is inherent in man to take sides, one can't help it. I know inherent is a hairy old word, never used in a permissive society. I'm dragging it out of the dust-bin.'

'Put it back in the dustbin where it belongs, Robert. If you want to know, I'm on both sides. We must, somehow, Robert, break it up. Render the whole plan on both sides ineffectual, send our Orange friends back home on the rickety boat and wreck Roundstone's neat little espionage service, which seems a pity since it seems to work marvellously well.'

'I suppose that their work has accounted for their knowing at least something about the various espionage services there are over the landing from the sea of illegal explosives.'

'Yes. I must say, we've become firm friends, they and I, after I had told them I had heard their talk from my parlour window. They have explained how the ships bringing explosives from America and from Europe make their journey almost as though they were on a motorway, that is, the way all the other ships come and go, *until* they are just so far from the land to which they are aiming. The various ports of landing operations are only decided upon when the operation is actually *on*. So you must do some thinking from now on, I've done the preliminary thinking with these three chaps dropping bits of information out of the sides of their mouths, like dirty eaters. Now it's over to you.' And she appeared to snuggle comfortably into her chair and look expectantly at him.

Robert walked up and down the room and wore an important frown. This seemed to him so very far removed from the centuries-old problems he was accustomed to:

> We fortify in paper and in figures,
> Using the names of men instead of men

(which bothered even Shakespeare) and the modern ergonomics – the scientific study of the relationship between man and his working environment – simple in comparison with the idea of following, spying upon and finally catching in the act of receiving a telephone message, probably in code, from a person connected with the ultimate destroying of human beings and mostly innocent ones at that.

He came across and sat on the bench beside the table, sliding closer to Nesta, pushing the glass away, turning towards her and holding both her hands, searching her face.

He could not say: Nesta, I have two frightful problems on my mind; one, I am suspected of being a murdering rapist, and second, the family I have deserted are, maybe, in some trouble for which they need me urgently. These two things are my first concern. I cannot possibly involve myself with the problem with which you are presenting me. I simply do not know what to do about it, or how to behave with regard to the problem.

When he got to know Nesta much, much better he would realize that the swift swinging of one leg, crossed over the other, was a sign that she was exceedingly concerned with the subject being discussed and was not going to drop it. No matter what.

And the police van arrived; they were making their now daily short call which amounted to surveillance, nothing less. They repeated the same questions in an admirable variety of wording. Robert stood upon the doorstep and talked to them from there, he had decided there would be no more silken dalliance with drinks. He played it their way but only up to a point.

'No, I have not yet come across the victim's basket of trinkets and shells. No, I have spent some time thinking about it but no idea has so far occurred. Yes, who knows, I may think of somewhere it might be. No, I did not go to the funeral, as you must know since you were surely there yourselves. (Neither am I the dog returning to its vomit.) No, I have not committed the fatal mistake always made by a murderer either. No, I would not know how to strangle anyone and nor, it would appear from the evidence at the inquest, did the actual strangler at the time. I gather it was an amateur job! No, I am not trying to be funny. Good afternoon, then, gentlemen, see you tomorrow!'

Coming back into the living-room where Nesta was still sitting in the rocking-chair rocking gently, he picked up *The Times* from where it lay, quite a distance from her, with the call for him shrieking at him silently from the Personal Column on the back page. Gently, and as though absent-mindedly and unconcerned, he turned it over to

the front page and neatly folded it there, with the name of
the paper written large. He stooped and shoved it
alongside the discarded newspapers on a shelf below the
cooking unit in the kitchen end.

And as he stood up, far from not catching the watchful
eyes of Nesta, once again he could not tear his eyes away
from her. Without speaking, somehow, they could say 'so
much and so much' to one another.

Even if she had seen it . . . the notice in *The Times* would
mean nothing to her, why should she connect it with him?
She could not connect it with him and that was that.

And now they could hear Roundstone coming up the
bank, playing his tune; it was a warm evening, the two
front doors were standing wide open and he stood there
waiting to be invited in. Robert was always pleased to see
that twisted rueful smile and that shiny brown beak.
'Come in, come in.'

'Ah, so Nesta's here, is she? You haven't been at your
easel these last days, dear Nesta, I have not seen you for
ages. It is time the subject of you as a strangler was
changed, Robert, we need to change it! The trouble is . . .
the police think they know who did for Biddy Hallow; in
fact, they don't think, they *know*, but they can't find one
blessed clue to pin on to you, Robert, or on me. Now, I
can tell them where Biddy's store of shells and bits and
bobs in her basket is, but I'm not going to.'

'For God's sake, man, if you know anything, anything at
all, tell them.'

'They'd test every shell for finger marks.'

'All the better! I'm serious, Roundstone.'

'But what about the day she was up here on that
donkey and all those picnickers saw that slight struggle
with you? Did you not touch any of her shells then, if you
remember?'

'God! You're right. I bought a box or two but in the
scuffle at the end I stood on them. What about you? Have
you touched any of the shells or objects in the basket?'

'You bet I have not!'

Nesta sat, moving slightly, listening but saying nothing.

Roundstone walked across to her and looked down: 'What's up?'

'A lot,' Nesta said. 'There's a lot wrong, Roundstone, and I wish you'd go.'

'Aw, why, girl?'

'I . . . I just wish you'd go.'

He went over and looked up at Robert. 'What's wrong with the girl?'

'The same as is wrong with us all, since you've asked me.'

'And that?'

'You feel it too, you know all about it; we're in a state of suspense and we will continue to be until certain matters have been resolved, let us say.'

Nesta looked across at Robert. 'I've known him a much longer time than you, Robert, so I shall take it upon myself to say what I feel I must say, now that he wants to know, obviously, what is on our minds.' But the tone of her voice was questioning and she looked up at Robert with raised brows. Then she said: 'If . . .' Then started again: 'What have you to do, if you're a priest, to get yourself sacked?'

Roundstone groaned and swung aside but he chopped the discussion off short by saying loudly, indeed by crying out with a bitter cry: 'You have to get found out to be an anarchist, that's all . . .' He turned on his heel and walked out into the sunset. They heard the sound of his steps on the gravel receding but they did not hear the accordion which he had left on a window-sill.

'. . . and I have not yet been out in his boat!'

'I think you should go.'

'Why?'

'Oh, Robert, I think to do so may cause him to tell you the truth about himself. He's told you about his boat-building business, and the foreman who died, and the wife and daughter who left him and the wife's work as a buyer in a London shop and daughter, etc., etc., etc. Simply ad libbing. The finding of the baby in the font in Manchester is more likely, and Father Jether is the most convincing of all because he has never denied it *or* admitted it. It's not the sort of name you invent suddenly. This lot, I've been telling you about, from long-ago hearsay, know him as Father Jether and you can't tell me he made that up!'

There was yet another long pause. Robert slumped down on the bench beside the table, elbows on the table and head between his fists.

'And come to that, Robert, who are you? Who are you?' Nesta asked coolly. 'I'm not asking you to tell me but I must point out that so long as you do not tell us all who you *really are*, you are bound to be suspected. You're affronted that you are suspected of being a strangling rapist, but someone is . . . It's no good getting on your high horse and saying: "Of course it could not possibly be *me*." So who are you, who is so special he is innocent because *he says so*?'

She crept out, leaving the doors open as she had found them and he heard her starting up her Mini and driving away into the distance, back to Carrioth.

Back to Carrioth.

No. To the coastguard's station.

There was nobody there. It was a mild and milky evening in high summer; the workers had gone home. Nesta walked the few hundred yards to the lonely hut that was Roundstone's. She tried the door; it was unlocked. She went inside. The first thing she saw, which could not be seen from the window, was a large crucifix hanging over his bunk. She dismissed this to think about later and pulled out an old seaman's chest from beneath the sleeping bunk. There was absolutely nothing whatever personal in it that would not be found in the chest of any working man or in any other drawer or shelf in Roundstone's cell. It was a miracle of impersonal occupation. Nothing, nothing, nothing: no books, not even a Bible, no bottles of pills such as everybody is bound to have in their bedrooms, and most surprising of all, no correspondence of any kind, no brown OHMS envelopes containing communications in pompous, archaic and incomprehensible language (such

as: *This form has no pecuniary value*, and *attestor sign here*).
She found herself staring thoughtfully at a packet of
gentleman's paper handkerchiefs; she threw them down
irritably and left, slamming the door after her. He would
of course guess that someone had been snooping around,
but she did not care.

In the meantime, Banjo had been otherwise engaged in a
love-affair in the village of Carrioth, his anxiety for his
master in temporary recession. She was a huge woolly
sheepdog such as can be seen any day on a journey up the
moving staircase in any London tube station in picture
form, advertising something.

The harbour wall opposite Nesta's cottage which had been
used by people since it was built two hundred years ago,
for leaning on and contemplation, for sitting on and
gossiping, for bargaining on, for repairing small things on,
for selling seasonal things like strawberries on – the wall
served as a communal table, and though Nesta thought,
too late, that it would be fitting not to become too friendly
with the Orange gang, as she thought of them, she could
not avoid seeing them and they seeing her every time she
went in or out, with her Mini parked round the corner,
out of sight, and she had to keep up her interest even
though she now knew all she wanted to know, or nearly
all.
    She could not but realize that the new advice regarding
the engine that they had taken was proving successful;
there was an air of satisfaction about them, a feeling that
they might just possibly be moving on before long.
    The one called Mac caught her eye as she passed and
followed her the few yards to her front door. 'It's going to
be all right, they've found the trouble,' he confided.
    'You'll be off, then?'
    'Yes, we'll be off.'
    'Back to Ireland?'
    'Soon, but not until we've done what we came to do.'
    'What is that, then?'

He looked at her, searching, then puzzled. 'You know as well as we do.'

Nesta cleared her throat, she felt suddenly sick. 'You're not . . . I mean *seriously* . . . you'll find where the boat is hidden, when it *is* hidden, I gather, and destroy any gear for sending messages . . . kind of thing?'

'Yes, that's right, and if that sub-machine-pistol you happened to see happened to go off, well, too bad.'

She was forced to give the appearance of being amused. Then she started as though she had suddenly remembered something. 'One of these evenings Roundstone is taking out that famous man we have here, living up at that newly done up cottage which used to be the coastguard's station, remember? Robert Escrick Cravenhead . . . *Sir* Robert Cravenhead, he's known all over the world for . . . for some invention that I can't possibly explain. But take care, for God's sake, you don't hit him by mistake.'

'Taking him out in his boat?' The man Mac sounded incredulous.

'Well, why not?'

'Great Scott!' he exclaimed with disgust. 'We're not on a Sunday School picnic, you know. We mean business. It'll be just too bad if a friend of yours gets in the light.'

'He is a friend of mine but that's not what I had in mind, it was your own skins. Lots of people might sympathize with your aims, but when it comes to an innocent man, whoever he might be, simply brought along for the ride, getting injured or worse, you'd have an outcry against you as murdering monsters. You know you would. *Sir Robert Cravenhead* . . . he would be an intolerable loss to industry . . .' And hearing herself Nesta was near to laughter in spite of being intensely serious because, of course, she was going to sabotage the scheme. The Irish weren't the only people who could do that.

'I thought the name was Escrick?'

'It is, but he's incognito and uses that second name whilst he's here on holiday.'

'Now, Nesta. You're a good girl, we all think that. Don't spoil your good impression, fussing. Just fussing.

You've done your bit for us and we're grateful . . . I . . . if I was you, I'd keep out of it, love, from now on. You don't want to get yourself involved, do you, like some-one we won't mention by name, who's got herself ten years, no less, and had a baby in the nick, too!' He squeezed her upper arm, and went back to the *Colleen Bawn* whose engine was now snorting with energy.

So now it was no longer a matter of nattering with the natives. The Belfast men had all the information they needed; it was now a matter of action and quickly because they felt they had been hanging about quite long enough. A job like this should be done lightning-fast, no time wasted. If it hadn't been for that damned engine in the *Colleen Bawn* it could have been all over and done with by now; they had had to chum up with the locals in the pubs for information but it should have been a more com-pact scene altogether: in and out, the IRA – employed spy called Father Jether, who had been a constant irritation these past six years, exterminated, and the explosives-laden ships out there hanging about waiting for instructions and not getting them. So there must be no time wasted, the operation Red Sail must be proceeded with forthwith, while this gentle north wind blew out from the land and the sea was as mild as milk.

The unusually placid weather had its effect upon Roundstone too; St Swithin's was in three days' time and he knew how often the weather would change to pouring rain and wind just about that time. Suddenly the sea would be ranting and raging and the holiday-makers screaming with excitement as the waves roared up the sands after them and soaked them with spray as they climbed about the rocks under the cliffs.

He could still get his messages across to the ships, but the worse the weather the more risky it was; as autumn came there had always to be a great gap in his activities because the frequent storms became so severe that a little sailing boat could be blown among the rocks and battered to bits in a matter of minutes.

For a long time now Roundstone had faced the truth
that an end must come; that he could not always be
relied upon to tell the munition-carrying ships where they
had to go. It was quite unbelievable that he had been able
to do so for so long without a hitch, he was convinced
utterly that the good Lord was on his side, helping him.
But he also knew that this same Saviour deemed it wise
to apply doses of bad luck as well as good to his servants.
Roundstone had come to terms with the belief that his
marvellous good luck had lasted an unusual length of
time and was due to run out any time now, hence his
recent serious conversation with Robert Escrick regarding
the disposition of his worldly goods. The very fact that
there were three hard-faced Orangemen now staying at
the village pub made him realize that he must use something which for all these seven years he had kept in
readiness to use in case of need, and it was a gun.

'Tomorrow night I shall take you out fishing as I have
promised, yes?' he said to Robert.

And Robert said: 'Supposing a mist comes over,
suddenly, in the way it does?'

'Then it's off.'

'What about half a gale blowing up suddenly, or even a
whole gale? I haven't experienced that yet, but I'm told a
lot about it from one and all.'

'Then it's off too, of course.'

'Right, then I'll meet you . . . where?'

'Down there on the beach, eight o'clock.'

'And I can't bring Banjo?'

'No,' Roundstone said crossly, 'we can't have him
aboard!'

'One minute.' Robert remembered something. 'You
were telling us you know where that blasted basket of
shells is. Last night when Nesta was here you said you
could tell the police but you were not going to. Why?'

'Why? Think of the trouble it would start – Biddy and
her shells. There is no one for miles round who has not
handled those blessed things some time or another. She'd
hold them up in front of people's faces and they'd have

to touch them. The Parson himself would be involved; there'd be somebody's fingerprints telling the tale, bound to be.'

'Well, fingerprints apart . . .'

'You can't put it that way . . . Biddy Hallow and her basket of shells are one thing, not two. Whoever strangled her was out of his mind to take the basket of shells away with him; must have been a total ass. What did he want them for?'

'Why the hell can't you tell me where they are?'

'Because, Robert, I think . . . they are as well there, where they are, as anywhere. They cannot do much harm, where they are.'

'Then you don't want the culprit, this gruesome strangler . . . found?'

Roundstone was quiet for some time while Robert glared at him, forcing him to keep to the subject. 'Perhaps you're right. As you're the chap they suspect, I should agree with you. Well, Biddy Hallow's precious basket and the contents are with the diddicois at their present camp, which is in one of those big dents you sometimes see on the moors, just enough to offer a bit of shelter from the west wind but not a permanent camping place, of course.'

'And where is that, for God's sake?'

He laughed. 'I hope you're not going to set out to find it yourself, Robert. It's up by the telephone-box.'

'Of course not. But the police are due here again at any time. I'll tell them, of course!'

'You needn't tell them I told you.'

'Of course I won't.' Robert pondered, then said: 'Still, it doesn't make sense to me, if the basket were found in the diddicois' camp, surely they'd be suspected?'

'They might well; it's the obvious conclusion, isn't it? But if you knew them as well as I know them, all these years, you'd realize . . .'

'Realize what? That they make very fine clothes-pegs?'

'Their way of life makes them obvious suspects, but you rarely get a gipsy in a court of law. I don't say never, but seldom, and the same applies to these second-class gipsies. I'm not saying the police don't suspect them; they naturally treat them the same as others; they'll search the camp, of course, but they know they're not going to find hidden treasure. Two nights ago, well after midnight, somebody was crashing about the camp and crashing is the word, everybody heard him falling about, they thought it was one of their own, come home drunk. It was. In the morning he had a shocking hangover. Either he won't say he found the basket, or, more likely, can't. But he had been in Carrioth and walked the five miles back, taking short cuts across the scrub. He didn't get home till two, they say, because the tide was in. I know all this because I was up there telephoning as I so often am in the summer.'

'You seem pretty familiar with these second-rate gipsies, as you call them.'

'I am. That telephone-box is about the remotest one in Cornwall . . . nobody uses it but me or the odd motorist from time to time.'

Roundstone stood up and put down his empty mug which had had cider in it this time. 'Listen, Robert, try to bear with me. You happen to be the only responsible person I have met in seven years with whom I can confide my . . . what shall we call it? IRA spying activities, if you like. A run of seven years with no major hitch is good, but it'll come to an end soon, I'm sure. The Irish war goes on and on but not for ever. Furthermore, those paupers called the Post Office (millions in the red) are closing down what they may consider unnecessary telephone-boxes, and the one up there is bound to go. It's two miles further than the coastguard's station, so there has to be two miles of overhead wiring, and though it was put there for the convenience of motorists, there's much less traffic now than there was. As I said, it's only used by me!' He laughed, saying they wouldn't like it if they knew what it was used for.

'And so . . . I feel the end is nigh and the best way of fending off bad luck is to discuss it in detail. The worst of bad luck comes suddenly. If you discuss the possible bad luck in advance, you may keep it off. Aren't I a superstitious old ass?'

There was nothing Robert felt like saying but there was something more that Roundstone had to say, since it had not been mentioned for so long he might have thought the people in the district had forgotten, but he was wrong.

'I know you want me to go, I know I'm boring you . . .'

'You're not, as a matter of fact . . .'

'But most of the things I told you *were* lies. Except about the provenance of my birth. They were what I would have *liked* to be the case; the boat business, my family. I had no business or family, no people that belonged to me at all. I was God's gift to the Catholic Church; they rescued me from the font, quite literally. So I was in it, theirs for life, cared for, educated, the lot, on their money, of course, because there wasn't any other. As I passed from the twenties into the thirties I became my own man. I questioned the humble priest with the shaved crown which they had made of me.

'Well, I became an anarchist, and that is another story; I had to be in this fine old monastery in County Kerry where I was sent after ten years in Rome. But it couldn't happen, you see. It's a centuries-old establishment, a favourite with the Holy Father in Rome himself. They couldn't do with me as an anarchist. In the kindest possible way, they quietly let me go, when my hair had grown. They sent their very best wishes with me and a hundred pounds, and after a bit of looking round, I came here, to Cornwall, mostly because the nearest Labour Exchange was so damned decent to me. I loved the coast then and still do, and when I came walking into Carrioth village the first thing I saw was the Shaven Crown . . . it seemed an omen . . . But they heard I'd joined the IRA and sent a package of holy monks here, after me; it made no differ- ence – I sent them away after a long long discussion and argument.'

Robert neither moved nor spoke; he did not want to miss anything nor did he wish Roundstone to stop until he

had really finished saying what he clearly had to say,
what he had long wanted to say. If never again, this was
now the moment of truth. What he said now could be
believed; what he had said before could not.

He said: 'When I was in the monastery I felt I wanted
to kill, and shoot and maim an amorphous enemy, even as
I prayed and prayed that I should be saintly, but when I
came out and had time to think instead of to pray all day
and part of the night, I discovered that violence is not what
anarchy is. I have my own definition of anarchy and I've
told you it. What it has boiled down to, these seven years,
is simply the old Irish question, *all* of Ireland for Ireland
. . . boring, really, and now I'm a part-timer working for
this aim I don't have to kill anybody, I only have to help
provide the bangs that kill others. So, Christ! what sort
of man am I? Even the seagulls despise me.' He took
the round stone out of his pocket and stared at it, as he
so often did, as though he found some truth there. He
tossed it slightly, throwing it up and catching it. Then he
replaced it in his pocket. He waited for Robert to comment and Robert did not do so because it was simply not
possible for him to say anything relevant until he had
thought the situation over.

'Right then, see you this evening,' Roundstone said, and
Robert could hear his receding footsteps on the gravel.

CHAPTER XIV

FRED BEDFONT and his young mate of Messrs Brown &
Bright, builders, were having their ten o'clock lunch-
break; Fred was repairing some bookshelves in the library
of a small town not far from Carrioth. The day before the
two detectives who had been working on the case of
Biddy Hallow were taking fingerprints and had got
round to Brown & Bright, who had been the builders on
the site at Zoygate near where Biddy's body was found.

Fred Bedfont would make a joke out of anything, funny or not; he allowed his fingerprints to be taken while making an unfunny running commentary and when it was over he said: 'Come along now, kiddies next . . .' and brought forward by the scruff of his neck Billy Bacup. It was sailing far too near the wind because Billy had done his stint in a detention centre, his main crime being a leader in teacher-bashing. However, this was three years ago and in the meantime Billy had developed good looks and a charm of manner which made everyone forget his past. He had achieved the manner of one almost breathless with the desire to please; he was a favourite with the men at Brown & Bright.

In the summer they knocked off work at five in the evenings and at four in the winter, which gave them time to get home in daylight and Billy had a most satisfactory way of starting to tidy up about three o'clock, and tidy up he really did, up to the last piece of chewing-gum stuck on the window. It was heartening to find that, after the tea-break, most of the tools had been tidied away so that there was nothing much to do before going home.

This benefit did not extend to Fred Bedfont who was considered a nut case since he slaved away energetically till several minutes after the hour for knocking off, with Billy Bacup slaving after him with a long-handled broom.

Jack Wither, looking down the list the police showed him, of those who had had their fingerprints taken, remarked:

'Billy Bacup isn't on it.'

'A school leaver,' one of the detectives explained.

'But the year before last . . . wait a minute . . .' He went off to consult the register, returning with Bacup's card. 'He's just turned seventeen, as a matter of fact. Go on, you take his fingerprints . . . there's no one you can leave out these days, except, perhaps, a kid in a pram.'

'And the ladies.'

'So you reckon women aren't stranglers?'

They left his remark at that, but they did say that

fingerprints were not going to be any good unless they found Biddy Hallow's basket, otherwise it was all a bit of a waste of time, since strangling doesn't often reveal finger marks on the flesh.

'What the strangler should have done,' Jack Wither said quite seriously, because he had evidently had this wilful murder very much in mind, 'was, dig a hole and bury the body.'

'Yes, but if you're going out on the sandhills with a girl, you don't often take a spade,' one detective said very soberly.

'Nor is the murderer going to leave the basket on the sandhills. He could have driven off in his car and dropped the basket anywhere between here and kingdom come!'

'The high road is not more than a couple of hundred yards from where the dead girl was found. So you see,' the other pointed out to Jack Wither, 'we have our problems, in case you're wondering.'

They were leaving but Jack Wither had something he must say: 'I'll tell you something; if there was only one man left out of the whole population and it was that good old Robert Escrick . . . it wouldn't be he I would suspect!'

Jack Wither had finished with them; he was busy. He murmured, just to get rid of them: 'I'd go to the school next and look through the school leavers, they seem a murdering lot to me . . .'

Driving away in their police car they laughed but one of them said: 'Why not? It might do them good to have us there on business. That new young chap teaching physical training was half killed last week, had to go to hospital, so I'm told, to have a crick in his neck put right, he got it in an attack on him in the gym!'

So they spent the rest of the morning in the senior section of the school to which the children of Carrioth went by bus. No good seemed to come of it, but then, no bad came of it either; when the parents heard that the search for Biddy Hallow's strangler had expanded to the seniors in the school they were impressed rather more than depressed. 'It won't do any harm,' was the consensus of opinion.

Tomorrow he would reply to *The Times*'s cry for Robert Cravenhead.

For five days now Robert Escrick Cravenhead's name had appeared in the Personal Column and Robert supposed they would complete the week and then a pause, then another week of printing the same, and so on, *ad infinitum*, until there was either an answer or a report that his body had been found. It weighed upon Robert heavily; he could not sleep, he could not eat with enjoyment.

Since a decision had to be made, Robert had decided what he would do. He had an old friend who lived in the Dordogne and had written a successful cookery book; he had been to stay with him twice, he had indeed considered the idea of going there himself but had decided against it because it would not have been the entirely new life he had been planning. But he had been on excellent terms with this friend whom he now felt was the only person who would not consider Robert's planned disappearance in the light of a selfish and childish prank, only to be jeered at. Tomorrow he would write to him sending a cutting of the agonizing cry in the Personal Column, (it used to be called the Agony Column, he remembered) and asking him to write a short formal note to his elder son Thomas asking if there was any bad news which his father should know about. Only that way could the ghastly stabs from his conscience be ameliorated or even stilled.

That would be tomorrow.

Tonight he was going a-sailing with his friend Roundstone and all would be revealed. At least, that is what he was expecting.

Nesta was having great trouble with her sympathies now. At first, when she had called on Robert, weeks ago, and he had shown her his domain she had, as everyone interested in books does, looked at his books on his newly arranged bookshelves while Robert was preparing a drink for them. He was talking and she was answering, but while it was going on, she was taking out a book here and there that interested her, looking through it, and returning it to the shelf.

On the first page of one or two of them there was a fine book plate and woven amongst the ivy motif was ROBERT ESCRICK CRAVENHEAD in emotive lettering.

It was as easy as that. Robert had not thought about his book plates for some time; three years ago they had been given him for Christmas by his secretary, who had worked for him for ten years, and he had enthusiastically stuck half of them in some of his books.

So last week, when he had left *The Times* upon the table, folded to the back page where the advertisement in the Personal Column shouted at her: *Sir Robert Escrick Cravenhead*, she took steps and had bought a *Times* for herself and had written to the solicitors who had advertised, signing her name and giving the London address of her flat in which her parents lived, saying that she knew the address of Sir Robert Cravenhead and she would undertake to see that any correspondence was re-addressed to him.

And that was all. She had thought about it long and carefully, in spite of all the other problems she had on her mind, and she had decided that to do this must be the right thing. She believed that this man whom she admired immeasurably, and liked immensely, was the victim of overwork. She did not even try a guess at his private affairs; she thought that his work had, now when he was nearly sixty, sickened him with the awful problems borne by management in industry over the last few years; the sinister change of heart in the working men who had served faithfully and loyally since time remembered.

So now, while awaiting results from her action, her main concern was to get rid of the visitors in the *Colleen Bawn*, because their presence here in Carrioth got badly upon her nerves.

The man who had finally overcome the engine trouble of the temperamental *Colleen Bawn*, who had come from ten miles away and who had come in his own speedboat, evidently asked a fair amount of money for his services and his departure was delayed because he needed cash payment, refusing a cheque for income tax reasons.

He had a married sister in the village, and when the *Colleen Bawn*'s owners complained that the banks in the nearest town would be shut until Monday, he said quite firmly that he would stick around till then and in the meantime the speedboat bobbed and bounced in the cross current at the harbour mouth and Nesta, later in the evening, heard him, after a session in the Shaven Crown, grumbling loud and long about Irishmen and their unpredictability and using freely the word, 'hammerchewer' which, when she woke up in the middle of the night, she was able suddenly to translate into 'amateur'.

Next day the movements of these 'hammerchewers' were diffuse.

Nesta had a job to do ten miles away but she decided it would be better to stay around for the present. She pulled on her old painting smock, took her pastels and easel, and started on a scene of the harbour which she had done several hundred times. She was well within earshot of the *Colleen Bawn* but today there was complete silence in the tiny cabin, and towards midday Mac emerged and soon reappeared in the car they hired for a day at a time.

There were voices now to be heard and presently he emerged from their boat once more and drove off, and while he was away, there was some hammering.

What was perfectly clear was that there was something going on of an unusual nature and there was that in the atmosphere which was causing a slight shaking in Nesta's stomach. She turned her painting pad upside down on her easel and took her chalks into her cottage. She went round into the main street and got into her Mini. She drove along the coast road, past the entrance with the broken letter-box to Zoygate, and stopped some two miles further along above where she knew that on the beach below, Roundstone's boat would be bobbing gently on the ebb tide.

Or she hoped so.

She ran far enough down the cliff path to make sure that it was; she felt like a fussy old hen in a state of anxiety about she knew not what. She drove back to Carrioth but still she shook slightly inside. She would watch that boat, the *Colleen Bawn*, until it sailed. She looked closely at her map, making sure of the direction the boat would take if it were returning to Belfast.

Tonight Robert was going a-fishing with Roundstone, the simplest of events, but Nesta was sick with unease. She had had attacks like this before, but usually when the cause of her anxiety was resolved she sighed with relief and abused herself for misuse of imagination.

She made a sandwich and re-seated herself at her easel. She watched the comings and the goings; she saw Mac return, she watched him go into the village street and return presently.

She assumed that the cash had now been satisfactorily handed over because soon the owner of the speedboat came round from the main street and leaned over the harbour wall, smoking a short pipe.

Mac returned and some angry shouting came from the *Colleen Bawn*. It was silenced almost at once. The sun shone fitfully; she was only pretending to be an artist at work because the light was impossible. She was going to go on 'painting' till dark, or until the *Colleen Bawn* had sailed away, if, indeed, she would go tonight. It was far more likely that the boat would sail early in the morning, because Mac and one other of his companions together carried out the box that was familiar to her, not large, and placing it with care in the back of the hired car, they drove off.

And now there was a shower of rain and Nesta was obliged to collect her things and retreat indoors, but she was still able to see almost as much as she could from her easel on the beach. Better, in fact, from her bedroom window. She raged when the telephone rang three times, each time with quite irrelevant and unnecessary messages.

Three hours passed, it was now seven-thirty, the hired car returned, one man got out carrying the box clearly which he threw carelessly down on the wall, discarded. He got back into the car beside Mac and they drove round the corner.

Returning the car to the garage, Nesta thought. And now? Meeting their chum in the Shaven Crown for a final meal? She went round to the Shaven Crown with her jug for stout. Yes, they were there, in the further room which was used for snack meals; she could see them through the glass door apparently celebrating, with pint mugs and laughter.

Back in the harbour the engineer who had repaired the engine of the *Colleen Bawn* was examining the box that had been left, apparently discarded carelessly on the harbour wall.

Nesta went up and stood beside him. 'Is that mine?' she asked, simply as an excuse for talking.

'Eh?'

'Just wondered if . . . it's rather like one I have.'

It was a lightweight plywood box lined with tinfoil and with a metal edge, the lid of which had been hammered down but was now simply lying on top. He had lifted the lid and sniffed and now he did it again, with Nesta at his elbow.

He obligingly held off the lid and putting the empty box close to Nesta's face he invited her to smell the inside.

She did so.

'Smell anything?'

'Yes. Yes, but what?'

He held the box to his face again. 'Can't think for the moment.' He sniffed. 'Smelt it in the Army.'

'Oh, what is it?' he cried to the darkening, clouded sky. 'What the hell is it?'

'Something eatable?' Nesta suggested.

There was another long pause, punctuated with sniffs,

then he struck his forehead with the front palm of his hand.

'Christ!' he turned to Nesta with shocked face: 'Christ Almighty!'

'Explosives?'

He nodded.

Excessively pleased with himself, Banjo had returned from his love-affair and every time Robert looked at him he grinned from ear to ear and wagged his tail inordinately, as though telling his master what spectacular pups he and the lovely bitch would have. As he was going without Banjo to meet Roundstone at his boat on the shore at eight, Robert took him a long walk, not along the shore but inland into the golden gorse country. He took his stick, stabbing it energetically into the ground and, as always when his mind was freewheeling, worded his letter to Angela. The pain he felt was not the dear pain of her remembered face; it was the shame of his own reluctance to write to her at all. He had humiliated himself, put down his burden and attained a spurious freedom. Like a child who opens his Christmas parcel too soon. He did everything that was required except, perhaps, the most important thing, writing to tell Angela. As time passed and he failed to do what he knew he should and must do, more and more words of self-abuse occurred to him, but alas, no words to explain himself to his once dearly cherished wife, and his awful lack of response to *The Times* cry for help.

On the way back from the walk with Banjo he had to cross the road to his own entrance and he flipped open the lid of the shabby letter-box as he passed. The letter was addressed in Nesta's own hand to Sir Robert Cravenhead and contained a letter from the solicitors in the Strand to Mrs Clare in London thanking her for the information regarding Sir Robert Cravenhead. It also contained a letter with a Sardinian stamp to Robert at his old home and was readdressed to the solicitors, unopened, in the handwriting of Robert's elder son.

May 30th

My very dear Robert,

This is going to be a big shock to you and I am sorry.
I am really sorry, dear, because I don't want to hurt
you. But I have a feeling that I won't be hurting you
as much as all that. I have left you because I have met
someone else whom, at my frightful age of 55, I am
potty about. Isn't it mad? He is not one scrap the man
you are but still the sight of him makes me go dizzy
and weak at the knees. So you see that's the sort of
woman you married, 37 years ago. At last it's out!

But we have grown apart since the children grew up
and I have been too occupied with entertaining and
being entertained and all that . . . things that, I
realize now, don't matter. So I am not coming back,
Robert, and you may divorce me. I shall go on living
with him at the above address which is his house and
home, and I shall lie in the sun and grow old grace-
fully, withering quickly with too much sun!

Don't bother about trying to forgive me, it's a waste
of your thinking time.

Angela

PS. I forgot to tell you, he's Prince Oradea (Olly), a
Roumanian, you met him once at the Durhams',
remember? He's been married three times.

Olly! Yes, he did remember him. He also remembered
Angela asking him on the way home how he liked 'that
dream-boat'.

He could not wait; he rushed back and snatched up his
writing paper. The hang-up he had had all these weeks
about writing to his wife, was, for the moment, over. He
must answer instantly unless his reluctance returned. He
put no address at the top but he wrote:

July 15th

My very dear Angela,

I have just received your letter of May 30th because

I have been living incognito for what you will rightly call
a selfish whim. Well, maybe, but I am happy. I had
better divorce you, not as a punishment or for spite or
anything like that, but because I have met a woman I
like very, very much. I love her too but liking is more
substantial than love, which I now suspect. I shall ask
her to live with me, and will leave it for a time to let her
decide whether we shall marry or not, but I should wish
to be free to do so.

Good luck, dear.

Robert

Olly! That creamy creep! How could you?

There was, of course, a great deal more to be said but
Angela was right; why tear themselves to pieces recapping
after all those happy years together? Together, they were
outlived and there were two fine sons and a lot (he
couldn't remember how many) of delightful grandchildren
to show for it. *And*, best of all, there were no hard feelings.

Before starting on this fishing expedition with Roundstone, he took the car and posted his reply to Sardinia at
the nearest village which was not Carrioth; the mystery of
his disappearance was now broken down and the Philis-
tines would be upon him with a tide of unwelcome letters
marked OHMS and many other unacceptable communications. His self-imposed experience of being entirely
alone had not been without value, however.

Mysterious though they are, diddicois must have, like
other people, water. Thus, they never break new ground
for their camps, they always go where there has been a
camp since before 1066 and all that. Unless there has been
a gun emplacement in 1940 and a with-it local council,
anxious to please, has obligingly piped water to it for the
convenience of the gunners.

They do an immense amount of washing, not because
they are cleaner than everyone else but because they wish
the result of their industrious washing to be an instant
proclamation that They are There and for the time being

This is Their Territory and not to be confused with a dairy herd or anything like that, even an outdoor jumble sale.

This dent in the surface high up on the Cornwall cliff did not attract robbers and thieves as such, but on this particular evening, when Robert was preparing to go out fishing with his friend Roundstone, young Bill Bacup was waiting for the light to begin to fail so that he could ride his motor-cycle up the steep, winding road to the diddicois' camp and retrieve the basket of shells, because they might well be used against him since the diddicois had declared, when Billy had questioned them earlier in the day, which was a Saturday and Billy not at work, that they were going to hand the basket to the police.

The diddicois knew, in the mysterious way they have of knowing things that happen on the beaches and elsewhere, who had strangled the wandering girl Biddy Hallow. They also knew that, as wanderers on the cliffs and shores, they were suspected by the police. This was something the diddicois had to put up with; they were always being suspected by the police and everybody else whenever there was an occasion for it. Though they were often guilty of misdemeanours on a small scale, it was seldom that any of them, in the whole wandering tribe, ever committed murder. So they wished to retain the basket, were careful not to handle the contents, and went to bed after hiding it in a bush under some indescribable washing, watched by Billy Bacup, his rosy, pleasant face taking on a mean look such as it rarely wore since he had completed his period of 'correction', lying on his stomach on ground slightly higher than the camp, his Honda motor-cycle concealed nearby.

He knew perfectly well that the police would hear from these people that one of them had actually seen Billy running fast away from the dead body of Biddy Hallow, but he also knew that that was not evidence, at least, not the only evidence that was needed in a court of law. Diddicoi evidence was not evidence, but it might have more credulity if the basket of shells were produced as well.

Billy was ambitious, he was just seventeen and he had learned at the correction centre more than many old lags. He knew that work must be avoided at all costs once one had grown to manhood. He was going to travel when he had succeeded in amassing enough money, and the first place he would visit would be Las Vegas. He would stay there a long time.

The tiny episode with Biddy on the sandhills annoyed him exceedingly. That day he was alone over the lunch-break with Fred Bedfont, and Fred would talk about the job they were on, making that single door into a double one at Zoygate. Fred was such a bore, Billy crammed his sandwiches down his throat with a drink of lemonade and two pep pills, and wandered off for a smoke of marijuana.

It was Biddy Hallow who started it, of course, when they met during that lunch-break at Zoygate, pawing him and mauling him and trying to cuddle him; you couldn't expect him not to start feeling sexy and then trying to have it off with her. Silly bitch.

It was not a question of he done Biddy Hallow, it was Biddy Hallow done him. If things went badly wrong and they accused Billy of strangling that female, it would be a big waste of time, a long step before he could escape into the good life. He was always doing sums in multiplication. Multiplying thirty quid a week to try to make out how many more weeks he would have to work in order to have enough money to start upon his adventure. He spent some time studying travel in the newspapers he came across, lying about or in the waste bins. They sometimes gave an idea of cost of travel by air to here and there, and he had a ragged atlas which he enjoyed studying too. He had looked forward to becoming seventeen, but now he had an uneasy feeling that the gaol arrangements would be less satisfactory than if he remained sixteen. There wasn't the slightest hope that Mum and Dad would give the wrong age, were the occasion to arise . . . with the police. And besides, his age was down on his record.

These were not new thoughts of Billy's; he thought them over and over again, it was a well-worn path. He had to lie here, in the brushwood, on his stomach until every sign of life in the camp had ceased, and as he lay he imagined himself on a beautiful soft round bed with a blonde on either side stroking him, while he ate chocolates out of an immense box of soft-centered only.

He was nearly asleep when a tremendous sound broke over him, the earth shook and the settling diddicois scuttled round like disturbed ants. Billy's teeth chattered momentarily with fright. Soon there was rising dust over the edge of the cliff between him and the setting sun.

In the meantime, down on the little harbour of Carrioth in front of Nesta's cottage, the mechanic who had repaired the engine of the *Colleen Bawn* tried to explain his alarm at the smell in the wooden box that stood on the wall between them to Nesta, shaken by his shocked expletives. Though the petrol engine had always been his first and last love, some years ago at technical college he had done a simple course in chemistry; amongst other elementary and, to him, useless information he had learned about *trinitrotoluene*, an explosive compound used at the present time in the manufacture of high explosive by the military and known as *TNT*. The reason it was so popular was because it could safely be melted at a fairly high temperature so that it could be poured into containers such as shell cases. But it was more commonly used in containers which looked like dry batteries, usually ignited by an electric igniting charge and blasting cap.

'There's been *TNT* in this box,' this bright young man declared, 'and what I can smell is old friend sulphuric acid.' He picked up a piece of wood from inside the box, about two inches long and an inch wide; 'And this is the wedge what they used to open the box with a wooden mallet.'

'So?'

'So if they're not damned careful that there *Colleen Bawn* of theirs is going to be blown sky high, and them with it.' And he demonstrated with raised hands and an impressive whizzing sound through his teeth. 'And it's not so clever of me to guess that they're off to blow up some-thing, it's a habit those Irish have. Let's hope they get themselves out of the way before it goes off.' He paused for a moment and added thoughtfully: 'They paid me OK with cash they wouldn't admit they had and gave me a drink; they're not such bad blokes, they're only a bit off their nuts . . .'

Nesta had vanished round the corner long before he had finished talking and had left her door wide open in her haste.

But the *Colleen Bawn* was out of sight, chugging peace-fully out into the westward sea, having got rid of the *TNT* by tucking the container into the covered space in the prow of Roundstone's boat, hidden loosely on this fine evening under Roundstone's oilskins and sou'wester, and timed to go off about nine. But you never knew quite . . .

As Robert set out to go on the fishing expedition with Roundstone, Banjo, of course, wanted to come too; he was more than usually elated after his three-day amatory exploits, his black coat shining as though he had just been polished, his brandy-coloured eyes pleasing, his tail wagging powerfully. He pleaded to come too, as he had pleaded on the morning his master left the old home for ever.

'Of course you can't,' Robert returned crossly. 'I'd like to take you, but just stay, STAY and keep off anyone who comes. STAY!' he shouted, looking back. In the ordinary way Banjo would have heeded the tone of his master's voice, but this evening he was so high-spirited that he bounded off to his own way down to the beach, still keeping an eye on his master and not believing, from his tone of voice, that this time he really meant – STAY. He knew the direction in which he was going, and would surprise him with his sudden presence when the walk was under way and thus irrevocable. Master would then be cross but only slightly, he could tell from the lack of con-viction in his manner this evening that he thought it a pity for him to miss a treat.

He kept his distance when, on the beach, he saw his master walking towards the coastguard's jetty, and Roundstone's boat, a familiar shape, lolled on the wet sand just above the water line of the receding tide.

Roundstone was struggling with the red sails. He and Robert greeted one another and Roundstone, looking past him, said: 'You've brought old Banjo!' Robert looked quickly round and a hundred yards off, there was Banjo, stopped now but smiling, with his tongue hanging out, his most endearing self. Robert shouted things like: 'Go back!' 'Go home!' 'Bad Boy!' and finally picked up a stone and aimed as though to throw it. But Banjo was not kidded by that old deception, he disappeared behind a rock while Robert and Roundstone dragged the sails up the wet sand to the mouth of the cavern into which, twice in twenty-four hours, the sea poured and roared for ever. They had put the sails up the cave as far as the dry sand so that the returning tide would not soak them, but the job was easy with two of them. At that highest point in the cave they let go of the burden, and as they turned the earth was riven with a god-awful explosion. Nesta had parked her car at the top of a path to the beach, she was tearing, slipping and sliding down the slope and from where she was could not see the boat, but was screaming to attract their attention. She only heard.

The bomb had been carefully timed to go off around the time when Roundstone was several miles out, but Banjo, terribly pleased with his manoeuvre to surprise and delight his master, squeezed himself into the space where he thought he would be concealed in the bows.

His master had been so astonished and delighted when he had emerged from the baggage in the back of the Range Rover on the removal day, and he expected a similar reaction ... why not? It was a matter of a big dog into a small space and in his effort to fit in Banjo pressed his front paw against the oilskin and upon the blasting cap with some force as he struggled under.

In a split second there was no boat and no dog but an

unthinkably loud hollow bang and an immense amount of litter spread over the wet sand and on the receding water's edge, and both Robert and Roundstone sprawled upon their faces, winded in the cave. Since the sails had not been carried in a straight line to the cave because the boat lay a short distance to the Carrioth side and was obscured from the cavern's mouth, the blast had not hit them directly, or they would both have been killed and, realizing this as they lay, they looked at one another in shocked astonishment that they had survived.

When they had recovered sufficiently Roundstone said that was it; their continued presence upon this globe was evidently unavoidable.

Later, when there were signs that Banjo had been involved, it was Roundstone and not Robert who wept. 'They've had it in for me these past three years,' he mourned, 'but I'm still here and you've lost your beautiful dog, Robert.'

Nesta was first upon the scene. She came flying down the steep path from the coastguard's station where she had parked her car and started her search for the two men. When she had thrown her arms round Robert and pressed her face to his, wet with tears, there was nothing to do but reassure herself that it was really he and there seemed nothing to say but 'Trinitrotoluene' every now and then.

People came, the police came, motor-boats approached from everywhere. There was nothing to be tied up because the next tide would wash about all the litter and the police search was only perfunctory while they waited for those who were involved to question them and others who had witnessed the explosion, if at all.

'Let us do it all tomorrow morning,' Robert suggested. 'Mr Roundstone and I are far too shaken to be coherent now.'

Nesta suggested she take Robert and Roundstone in her car back to Zoygate for a pick-me-up and Robert enthusiastically concurred. Roundstone, too, said he would like to come but there was something he had to do.

He pulled Robert's arm, taking him aside and telling him
that he must pick up his bicycle from the coastguard
station yard and ride up to the telephone-box from which
all his messages were sent and received and report that
his boat had been blown to smithereens. 'And sign off,'
Roundstone added, looking hard to see if Robert had
received the message.

Robert's face was none too clear in the dusk but
Roundstone was satisfied that he knew what was meant.
It was meant that Roundstone had had enough of his
work for the Sinn Fein, he would like to give it up, and
as a new boat and equipment would be involved, now was
the time to finish.

Leaving the crowd on the beach, together the three
walked silently up the steep path to the station yard and
Roundstone pulled his old bicycle out of the shed; he
stood for a moment in front of Nesta and Robert as they
were about to get into Nesta's car.

'I'm strangely happy,' he said. 'Banjo had a messy end
but he never knew what hit him. He died happy in the
knowledge that he was, by this last act, pleasing his
master!' He reached forward suddenly and clasped
Robert's hand as he leaned across his bicycle.

"'Tis safer to be that which we destroy
Than by destruction dwell in doubtful joy.

Eh, Robert? I've just discovered that!'

He swung on to his machine and as he rode off they
heard him singing the Gloria in plainsong, to the music of
Tallis, slowly and slowly.

Nesta and Robert had no words left; they gained strength
from closeness to one another as they lay silently on
Robert's bed, wrapped together until about seven-fifteen
in the morning when there was an impatient banging of
the dolphin knocker upon Robert's door.

It was two men from the coastguard's station. There
had been a disaster of major proportions on the hill,
between the station and the telephone-box. They came

for the purpose of asking for any information they might have.

The diddicois had settled down again about three-quarters of an hour after the explosion the previous night; one of them having been sent down to the shore to report back with the news.

Billy Bacup had one object only in mind and he was getting madly restless. He crawled out of the scrub and, still on hands and knees, advanced to where the stolen basket of Biddy Hallow was hanging by a hook beneath one of the shabby caravans, where he had seen it hanging on his last visit, with a pile of rags covering it. He had brought some old plastic washing line which his mother had thrown out, and when he got back to where he had hidden his motor-cycle he tied the basket on the carrier at the back where he usually strapped his helmet when the machine was parked. Tomorrow early, being Sunday, he would take it away, he had not yet decided where, but miles and miles from anywhere. Nobody finding it would know whose or what it was because Billy planned to scatter the contents over a wide area.

This tiresome job now half done, Billy revved up his Honda excessively, not caring now who heard. Sheer exhilaration at the success of his foray made him step it up to fifty and he screeched down the sloping road and round the bends horizontally at fifty.

How could he guess that Roundstone was plodding his way up the hill on his bicycle, singing as he had done several hundred times on his way to the telephone-box, making it easier for himself by riding side to side. The Honda had its headlights on and Roundstone must have heard the machine coming, but it was going so fast it was cutting the corner and on its wrong side and caught Roundstone as he was jerking his old bicycle into the ditch for safety, out of the way. It caught him full on and his chest was crushed.

The rider, Billy Bacup himself, went flying head over heels, landing on the hard surface of the road on his head, fifteen feet further on. 'Roundstone's dead and the boy, no one knows who he is yet, said to be dying,' they reported. And the horror, or rather the additional horror, was that they had lain like that in the road all night until one of the staff on the way to work at six-thirty a.m. had found them.

So Roundstone had had a miraculous escape from death by being blown to pieces only to be savagely killed as he rode slowly along the uphill pull, thanking heaven for his deliverance. If he was?

There were still things to be done about Roundstone. Robert and Nesta drove twenty miles to the hospital where the head of the coastguard's station had identified the body. He was still at the hospital mortuary trying to make arrangements for some kind of funeral and was glad to share his responsibility with Robert, who offered to take over since, he said, Roundstone was his friend.

But Billy Bacup was surprisingly not dead; he regained some sort of consciousness during the day but he seemed to be almost entirely paralysed and his parents and family stood in despair watching his attempts to speak.

Nesta stayed all day with the Bacup family, who badly needed someone with them to keep down the hysteria which kept breaking out between the mother and the father. The two sisters crept under a bush and hid for hours. Billy had been the family's hope of salvation, they were so proud of him, but he was so gravely injured that Nesta hoped he would die.

The whole situation of Billy Bacup was strange and harrowing in the extreme. Within a few days there was a complete case of murder against Billy. When working at Zoygate with Fred Bedfont for Messrs Brown & Bright, Billy had, as he often did, strolled away for a smoke after eating his snack in the lunch-hour. Fred and Billy had got on well together, Fred told the police; the boy was an enthusiastic worker and saving up carefully for some future ambition. But Fred would not tolerate constant smoking, gave long lectures about ruining lungs and wasting money, so Billy would steal off and have his smoke no matter what Fred said. And this he had been doing when he met the wandering Biddy Hallow with her basket of shells.

A nymphomaniac manquée, or wasted nymph, the Police Inspector referred to her as a 'public nuisance, pitifully malformed, she drove the kid to a frenzy!' Two of the diddicois saw Billy running away on the deserted sands area near Zoygate on the Carrioth side. Curious to see from what he was escaping, they went in the direction from which Billy ran. They found the dead girl and they found the basket of shell oddments a few yards away. They took it because they always took things they found. As time went on they decided to return it, just as they found it; their relations with the police were dicey, to put it mildly, they felt it safer to return the basket just as they had found it and were going to do so, on the better late than never principle. Billy had been to ask them if they had found it, and even as they denied it, he could see where it hung beneath the caravan.

After a time it was evident that Billy Bacup was destined to go on living. A great deal of money was and would continue to be spent on trying to revive his destroyed nervous system, but the boy remained inert and unable to speak so that anyone could understand him. It was impossible to charge him with murder or anything else. If one believed in retribution, there it was, all meted out to Billy for the crime of strangling Biddy Hallow who, in her pathetic way, enjoyed her life. Billy would never now lie on a round bed in Las Vegas with a giggling blonde on either side and a box of soft-centred chocolates.

But a totally crippled Billy did wonders for his Problem Family; from now on they devoted themselves to the poor cripple. They begged, in time, to have him back home, and as hospitals are always glad when a patient's people wish to have him at home, they bought much special equipment such as a bed, not a round one, but one fitted with all kinds of special pulleys, and the father and mother and two sisters devoted themselves to his care, his father going permanently on the dole and with several grants had ample money for everybody.

But Fred Bedfont had something on his mind which he would never, never, as a happily married man, have divulged in a lifetime had it not been for the ghastly double disaster on the road.

Long, long ago in May, when the new house for Mr Escrick was complete, there was one evening when Fred had stayed behind to improve the look of some woodwork edge, leaving Billy to get home on his motor-bicycle, he having his own car there. Biddy Hallow had simply walked in, or slithered in, in her slimy way. In short, he had assaulted her, as best he could, uncomfortably, in the new bathroom. He had no patience whatever with that nuisance, she'd no right to come in the house; he had fled, leaving her moaning, and that would serve her right. He lived in another village miles from Carrioth and Biddy only knew him by sight. He had been slightly upset to have to return for the alteration to the front door, but there it was.

He told the police this and they wrote a full confidential report of what he had to say, which was kept under lock and key for future use, if necessary. He had been in such a hurry to get away he forgot to lock the door and had subsequently thrown the key away.

But this did lead to the police deciding that Biddy Hallow was in a state of progressive dementia which would have led, fairly soon, to her being committed possibly permanently to a hospital for people of her kind. Latterly she had been far more insistent upon notice being taken of her and several complaints of her behaviour had been noted at Carrioth police station by Sergeant Crum.

Granny Hallow, cooking for the Parsonage couple, after her granddaughter's funeral, warned everybody that she would never speak of Biddy again so long as she lived and everyone considered her wishes.

HM Chief at the coastguard's station sent a note to Robert asking him to come. He showed him Roundstone's cell, as Robert called it. He gave Robert an envelope in which was the Will which Roundstone had had made, bought at a stationer's and witnessed by himself, the Chief, a month ago and in which he had left everything he possessed to 'Robert Escrick'. It was touchingly little. Roundstone had received the statutory pay for his work for the Admiralty, however humble, but he had sent all but enough to keep him in tobacco, fed and comfortable, to a monastery in County Kerry in Ireland, 'for the poor'. There was an account book in which these sums were entered week by week; they included the insurance money he was paid and the money he should have used for insurance stamps. There was also an envelope of small stick-on receipt slips on which were printed the address of the monastery, which Robert seized with pleasure.

He asked for permission to make the arrangements for the funeral, to pay for it and to do what he wanted with the casket, and this they were only too glad to hand over. He drove away with the accordion and the mouth organ in his car and the crucifix which Roundstone had hung over his bunk and the little round green stone in his pocket. And since the Chief had not been on the station long there was no comment made about the character of Roundstone. He remarked upon the explosion on the beach as being a tragedy but implied that there was no doubt a lot behind it, with which it was better not to 'interfere'; it was, anyway, nothing to do with HM Coast-guards, he was glad to say.

There was no trouble at the inquest. The explosion on the shore was discussed and it was decided that Round-stone, leaving the scene after the event at which he had narrowly excaped being blown to bits, was badly shaken and thus had not been able to save himself from the approaching Honda, as might have happened if he had not been badly shocked half an hour previously. The details of the explosion, such as they were, passed on to a higher authority.

Robert gave his name as Sir Robert Escrick Cravenhead

and said he had used the name Escrick his first three months at Zoygate only for personal reasons which no longer applied.

And then there was time to talk about themselves, Robert and Nesta.

He showed her Angela's letter and after she had read it over three times she laughed. 'I like her.'

'Everybody does, but up to a point. She stands for fun and games, and youth and the old thing *whoopee* which you will not have heard of. This Olly is twenty years younger than she is.'

'And I am twenty and more years younger than you.'

'Alas!' He stared at her thoughtfully.

'But I could never find a man like the one I had, Robert. If you were any younger than you are, I wouldn't ... *like* you as much as I do. You at nearly sixty are the person I like, just as you are ... the man for me now, and for ever after.'

And later Robert stood in front of the bookshelves and took out a book at random, laughing at the book plate and saying what an ass he was not to have remembered his anonymity and left the ones with his name in behind: that and his driving licence; how careless! And he had been so pleased with himself.

Nesta said, 'Nobody round here will even remember out loud that you were, even last week, known as the Raper.'

'You think not?'

'I know it. Your title having been established, no one would be so gauche as to refer to you ever having been a rapist. Never. They'll forget, too, your having started off your life here with this ridiculous charade of being someone else, or nearly so, but your manner at Roundstone's inquest was probably the old style you, as you used to be all your life. You simply stated that you wished to do this anonymity thing and that was it, no questions asked.'

'It seems so mad now,' he said sadly. 'Men of my age often do the most insane things, especially if they are on the edge of retirement; they lose their common sense. How long did I think I could live without anybody knowing my real identity? It was partly a cowardly fear.'

'Of what?'

'Of facing my family and telling them all that I did not want to see them again, I was tired of them. I was a coward and couldn't bring myself to do it. They would have thought I was sick and sent me to psychiatrists and asked nervously how I was, every other week . . .'

Robert brought Roundstone's casket of ashes in from the car and put it on the top shelf of his bookshelves. 'Soon,' he said, 'we shall go to Ireland and find this monastery of which I now have the name and address. I shall interview the Holy Father or whatever he's called and ask him if Roundstone can be buried there. He'll say not, but I shall insist. I may have to use money for it but I don't mind.'

'Why?'

'Because I would want him to admire and, in a brotherly-love way, love his ex-monk.'

'But he was wicked, Robert. His small activities were a personal act of war.'

'He was a good man. Much better than I, with all my worldliness. Remember what archy, Don Marquis's American cockroach wrote on his boss's typewriter?

> "It takes all sorts
> of people
> to make an
> underworld." '